Common Core

A Story of School Terrorism

Joel Spring

ISBN: 0615873545
ISBN-13: 9780615873541
Library of Congress Control Number: 2013948992
CreateSpace Independent Publishing Platform
North Charleston, South Carolina

Chapter 1

US Secretary of Education Paul Blanchard's head hit the edge of the lectern as he fell off the dais, landing with a thud on the floor in front of a horrified group of Ohio state education officials in Dayton. He'd felt nauseous all day but still wanted to give his speech on how the Common Core Standards as a framework for teaching subjects across the country would make the nation number one in the world's economy. He had just uttered the word "standards" when he collapsed. He was pronounced dead in the emergency room of Dayton's Good Samaritan Hospital. Later, the cause of death was determined to be ricin poisoning.

Unaware of the unfolding tragedy fifty miles north of them, two teachers sat in a stuffy storage room of Cincinnati's Booker T. Washington Charter School, carefully erasing wrong answers on the state required third-grade test and filling in the correct ones. Their principal, Carl Grinder, a tall, well-dressed, handsome black man in his late forties, had warned them that low test scores would close their charter school, which was squeezed between two tenement buildings in Cincinnati's Over-the-Rhine neighborhood.

"Jesus," Eric Somers blurted out to Blanch Cooper, who sat across from him, changing test scores. "After all the time on test prep, I can't believe they did this poorly. These kids can't do these state Common Core tests."

Eric, a pudgy white man in his early thirties with developing male pattern baldness, worried about losing his job and paying his student loans and house mortgage if the state shut down the school. He was sure his wife would take their daughter and move back to her family in Florida if they faced any more money problems. They were just scraping by on his $35,000 salary and the extra money he made working evenings bagging groceries in a neighborhood supermarket.

It was five at night, after students went home, when the two teachers began working on the test's Scantron answer sheets. The school's brochure promised parents to improve their children's life chances with a school day from 8:00 a.m. to 5:00 p.m. Or, as Carl told the teachers at the beginning of the school year, "These poor kids need more school time if they are going to keep up with rich kids."

"How are you doing?" Carl asked, joining the two teachers in the storage room. "Remember, don't make the scores too good. Just get 'em up to passing. The education department is going to be suspicious if it's suddenly a miracle at Booker T. Washington."

"They'll wonder if we give them acceptable scores. Failing and dropping out are all these kids do." Blanch Cooper looked warily at the principal. "These new Common Core tests are a disaster. Some broke down crying."

"Thank the test-maker, Brightstone," Eric said. "I didn't understand some of the questions, they were so poorly written. It's as if the company was trying to meet the state deadline by throwing anything together. I found one question that is the same as one appearing in the Brightstone text we're using."

"I heard kids were puking in other schools," Blanch added. "Imagine all the pressure to do well, and then the tests don't make any sense. The kids we've got wouldn't do well even if the tests were okay."

Like most whites growing up on Cincinnati's west side, Blanch harbored a deep belief in the mental slowness of the city's black population. She resented taking orders from a black principal. Like

Eric, she needed the job, being a single mom with two kids and an ex-husband who only occasionally paid child support. She ran her hand through her stringy, blond hair, causing white specks of dandruff to fall on the Scantron in front of her. In her middle twenties, she had inherited a thin body from Appalachian ancestors.

"We're here to save them." Carl recited the mission statement of the Booker T. Washington Charter School Network: "While traditional public schools fail to help disadvantaged students, the Booker T. Washington Charter Schools will provide individual help, focused lessons, character development, longer school days, and family outreach programs to ensure their students are prepared for jobs in the global economy."

Bunch of bullshit, Blanch thought. These kids are headed to jail.

Suddenly, Carl's secretary, Deborah Falk, another west side woman sporting a bouffant hairdo and wearing spandex pants with a loose blouse to cover her obese white body, burst into the small room, yelling, "You've got to see this on TV!"

"What?" Carl answered, irritated that the disruption might interfere with correcting student answers.

"The Secretary, Secretary of Education, he's dead, something about ricin. He was speaking up in Dayton."

* * *

The next morning fire trucks raced down Vine Street to the Booker T. Washington School. The explosion was heard across the river, in Covington, Kentucky. It tore through the fifth- and sixth-grade classrooms next to the storage room. Stunned and covered with dust, blood, and what later turned out to be human tissue, Principal Grinder stood across the street, watching his burning school. He'd been standing at the entrance to the school, giving some final instructions to his secretary, when the explosion occurred.

"Mr. Grinder, what happened?" asked his bloodied secretary, who followed him out of the school. "What about the kids?"

"School Explosion Kills 5," screamed the evening headlines of the *Cincinnati Reporter*.

"We don't know the cause," said a police official quoted in the news story. "The FBI, Cincinnati police, and fire officials are investigating. Homeland Security has been alerted because of a possible terrorist act that might be linked to the poisoning of the US Secretary of Education Paul Blanchard. All we know at this time is that the bodies of four children and one adult were removed from the rubble. The two adjacent apartment buildings were evacuated before any residents were put in harm's way by the fire. Seventeen children and three teachers are in critical condition in Cincinnati hospitals. Ten children are in the burn unit of the University of Cincinnati Hospital. Other students and teachers received minor injuries and were treated and sent home."

* * *

In Jinan, China's final preparations were being made for a demonstration of Kiwi's new teacher robot. One of the world's leading makers of smart phones, computers, and computer tablets, Kiwi worked with Brightstone to design and build a robot to replace human teachers. Booker T. Washington Charter Schools planned to buy the first batch of teacher robots to reduce cost and ensure control of the instructional program. Secretary Blanchard, prior to his death, was a major advocate for teacher robots.

"You don't have to worry about teacher robots screwing up lessons," Blanchard explained to his staff members in the Department of Education. "They'll stick to Common Core lessons and won't go off on tangents. Robots get to work on time, and they'll ease budget problems in local schools, since they don't require health insurance, pensions, and, except for minor maintenance, never use sick leave. Teacher robots taking over classrooms will save American schools and disadvantaged kids."

Chapter 2

"Oh, my God." Carl Grinder wept, sitting in the living room of his posh, four-bedroom apartment in the trendy Cincinnati neighborhood of Mount Adams. After a long night accounting for teachers and students and being interviewed by the police, he made it home around one in the morning and collapsed on the couch into the arms of his waiting wife, Cherry. They'd met at Yale, but didn't strike up a real courtship until they shared a conversation at a party hosted by his hedge fund at New York's Pierre Hotel.

Carl grew up in a wealthy family in suburban New York, graduated from Yale with a BA in sociology, and joined Harriet Kelp's Educators for the World. Kelp founded the volunteer teacher corps in the 1990s, believing that the best graduates from the best schools could save needy kids. He volunteered for Educators for the World, because he didn't know what else to do after graduation. A couple of years teaching, he felt, would give him time to plan his future. Educators for the World placed him in a fifth-grade class in a run-down school in Baltimore's poorest neighborhood. With only scant training at a ten-week summer session, he was unable to control his students and fumbled around for the two years, hoping he didn't do too much damage. He left the Baltimore school and joined a Wall Street hedge fund that also consulted on moving production from US plants to China. By his mid-thirties, he was worth over $50 million.

Cherry was invited to Carl's hedge-fund party after a striking photo of her appeared in the *Wall Street Journal*, announcing her partnership in a prestigious law firm. Seeing the photo and remembering how beautiful she looked as a Yale undergraduate, Carl added her to the invitation list, hoping she was still single. They married within a year in a festive and expensive wedding in the exclusive Hamptons. When Carl decided to quit investment banking and become a principal in Cincinnati, Cherry opted for a career change, tired of working for greedy stockbrokers. She took a position running Cincinnati's National Underground Railroad Freedom Center.

The phone woke them the next morning at eight thirty. It was a call from the local FBI office, asking Carl to come in around ten that morning for questioning. The night before, Carl had told police and reporters what little he knew about the blast. When asked by a TV reporter about the possibility of it being a natural gas explosion, he explained that the gas boiler had been shut down at the end of the heating season, and the gas line was closed.

Carl drove out to the FBI offices, located in a boxy glass building on the eastern edge of Cincinnati on Ronald Reagan Drive. After identifying himself at the front desk and passing through security, he was given a visitors badge and escorted to the second-floor offices of FBI Agent Tim Geary.

Tim was put in charge of what looked like a terrorist case because of his experience working on the 2013 Boston Marathon bombing. A tall, broad-shouldered white man in his middle thirties, with a scar running from his right ear to above the corner of his mouth, he had been an agent for almost a decade. Tim's size plus the scar made him an imposing man.

"Please, sit down." Tim pointed at the chair in front of his desk. "Must've been rough last night. Want some coffee?"

Carl declined, looking at the walls decorated with framed commendations, Tim's law-school diploma, and several photos of Tim at the Boston Marathon crime scenes.

"I got a call about an hour ago from the fire chief. He thinks the explosion, at least from the school's floor plan, originated in a storage room near the back classrooms. Anything explosive stored there?"

"It mainly held computer things, like tablets, laptops, and software. Plus, it was crammed with state tests and student answer sheets. We just finished the state tests."

"Do you have an inventory of the room? Or did it go up in the fire?"

"All records are stored on a cloud housed by our parent company, the Booker T. Washington Charter Schools."

"Our forensic team from the Boston Marathon bombing is flying in this afternoon. They'll figure out the nature of the explosion." Tim leaned over and turned on a recording machine in front of Carl. "I have a few questions. We may call you back for another interview. Shall we start?"

Nervously, the principal nodded he was ready.

"First, I want to tell you we've already collected a file on your life from our central data system. Since this may be a terrorist act, we've been given clearance to use the National Security Agency's database."

Carl felt a wave of panic, thinking of the porn sites he visited on sleepless nights, when he quietly slipped out of bed, not wanting to disturb Cherry.

"Let's start with some basic questions regarding the explosion." Tim sipped his coffee and opened a note pad. "I'll remind you that you're being recorded. I'm making notes for follow-up questions. First, do you know of anyone who might want to harm your school?"

"No, I can't imagine anyone blowing up a school dedicated to helping poor children."

"Does the school have any enemies? Has it ever been threatened?"

"No, except for the teachers union." Carl laughed. "They certainly hated our opening."

"Please explain. Why would the union be opposed to your school?"

"They picketed and marched around when we opened. They waved signs and tried to keep parents and kids from entering."

"Why?"

"We're a charter school." Carl sighed, thinking of the many conversations at the Yale Club about possible teachers-union opposition. "We don't have nor do we want the unions in our charter schools."

"I thought all Cincinnati schools were unionized." Tim made a note to interview the head of the local teachers union.

"We're a school chartered by the state, meaning we don't have to pay attention to local school district or union rules."

"Why would you want that?"

"We believe these poor kids need more time in school. Our teachers work from seven in the morning to five or six at night—much longer than the union contract with the Cincinnati schools."

"So the union is threatened by your long hours?"

"More than that: we pay less and have fewer benefits, in order to survive."

"Did the union ever threaten you about these issues?" Tim made another note to investigate teachers-union violence in other parts of the country.

"They screamed and yelled at me and my teachers during a week of picketing, when we opened. One swung a picket sign at me, almost hitting my head. Then there were the car problems."

"Car problems?"

"During the week of protest, the windshield wipers were ripped off my car. Some teachers had their tires sliced. One teacher's car was spray-painted on the front, sides, back, and top with the word 'scab.'"

"Did you report this to the police?"

"Yes; they didn't find out anything. The school had to pay for a secure parking lot for all our staff."

"Hm." Agent Geary turned on his computer screen, revealing Principal Grinder's data file. "I see you're wealthy and live in a very expensive apartment in Mount Adams—investment banking and overseas management, it says here."

"Made enough and decided to help kids and do something more interesting." Carl thought about the evening when he had sat in New York City's Yale Club, having drinks with two other investment bankers, Marvin Goldman and Abe Stein, planning the Booker T. Washington Charter School Network. They knew each other from being placed by Educators for the World in the same Baltimore school. "One thing I learned from my Educators for the World experience is that these poor kids need discipline," Abe had said.

"Your data file says you were involved in China with Kiwi technology. What's that all about?"

"Our firm helped companies relocate overseas to save money on labor. The Kiwi executives asked us to set up production in China."

"Our files show the Booker T. Washington Charter Schools making large purchases from Kiwi."

"Jesus!" Carl exclaimed. "How did you find out that much so soon? It hasn't even been twenty-four hours since the bombing."

"We can put a person's life together almost instantly—could make a movie of your day by piecing together security videos from street and store cameras. Did it in Boston with those terrorists. So, why the purchases from Kiwi?"

"Kiwi sells classroom tablets and software. There is a big demand for these products with the Common Core."

"Did you know the secretary of education was giving a speech on that topic when he was poisoned? By the way, what is the Common Core?"

"It's just guidelines adopted by states on how subjects should be taught. Math and literacy are the big ones."

"Tell me about Kiwi making money off the Common Core."

"Well, school districts don't have the time or money to have teachers align their subjects to the Common Core. The cheapest and safest way to ensure compliance is to buy Kiwi and Brightstone software to do the job. Brightstone makes the Common Core tests."

"And Kiwi tablets?"

"The tablets are loaded with readings and math lessons for the standards. They can download e-readings from Brightstone. Plus, the tablets can access the national student database, inBloom."

"You still own a large number of Kiwi shares, which is making money selling to your charter-school network."

Carl winced at the full realization that his whole life was an open book to the government. "Yes, I own shares, and I admit they are profitable. I'm selling them and putting the money into the Common Core Fund. It's an education investment fund."

"Do you think there is a conflict of interests, using state charter school money to buy products from a company that you make money from?"

"Never thought of that." Carl gulped. "I'm helping kids by giving them the best technology and learning tools."

Tim scrolled down his screen and made a couple of handwritten notes before asking, "What do you know about the riots at the Kiwi plant in China?"

Carl gasped. "You think Chinese agents blew up my school."

"We can't rule out anything, with a possible terrorist act. Tell me about the riots in the Kiwi plant."

Carl sighed, recalling his discomfort when first approached by Kiwi executives. "Kiwi came to us, saying there was money to be made in education by exploiting the Common Core. They knew their products had to be relatively cheap to sell to cash-strapped school districts."

"So they wanted to use cheap Chinese workers?"

"Yes. I went over and found an abandoned factory that was used to make herbicides to keep American lawns weed-free. It already had worker dorms, and we just had to redo the plant to make Kiwi products."

"And the riots?"

"Cramped dorm rooms housed twelve workers in triple-deck bunk beds. They worked twelve-hour shifts and could be awakened at any time if Kiwi wanted crash production on a product."

"Did they riot over those conditions?"

"It all started with suicides. Never thought of Chinese killing themselves; only thought of that as a Japanese thing."

"Why the suicides?"

"I was sent over to investigate. Kiwi was concerned with their image—they had built a strong following here and abroad with their innovative products."

"So, they needed a positive image to sell to US schools."

"Yes. What I found was poor working and living conditions. We hired a Chinese researcher to interview workers. He concluded the suicides were caused by despair that they would spend the rest of their lives in Kiwi dorms."

"And, what did you recommend to Kiwi?" Tim's face reflected his distaste for Kiwi's working conditions.

"I told them the causes of the suicide epidemic."

"And what did they do?"

"Do you think Kiwi had something to do with my school and the secretary of education?"

"I'm asking the questions," Tim quickly responded. "What did Kiwi do?"

"First, they had their public-relations firm draft a plan to ensure none of this hurt their image. They put up suicide nets around the dorm to catch any jumpers."

"Did the nets cause the riots?"

"Are you accusing China and/or Kiwi of terrorist acts?" Carl was feeling uncomfortable, knowing the FBI agent had access to data showing the money he was making from Kiwi's school sales.

"I'm not accusing anyone. We're investigating a possible terrorist act," the agent testily replied. "Just answer the question."

"The riots started when Kiwi introduced its new tablet and software aligned with the Common Core. The demand in the United States was so great, the workers were put on sixteen-hour shifts, and the riots broke out."

"Then what happened?"

"The People's Liberation Army was called in." Carl remembered being upset when he heard the news. His ancestors were slaves, and he thought of Kiwi's Chinese workers as slave labor.

"Why the People's Liberation Army?" Tim thought he should alert the State Department about possible problems with the Chinese government.

"Kiwi paid bribes to Communist Party officials to get the factory up and running. These officials didn't want the flow of money from Kiwi interrupted. They sent in the army and built fences around the plant, with twenty-four-hour guard stations."

Tim leaned back, staring at the ceiling for a few minutes. Straightening himself upright, he offered a summary of the conversation. "Tell me if I'm correct." The agent stared directly into the principal's eyes. "You and Kiwi are making money selling products related to the topic of the US secretary of education's speech when he died. Involved in this scenario is the Chinese Communist Party, the People's Liberation Army, and, of course, Kiwi. Is that correct?"

"Well, I wouldn't state it like that." Carl felt nauseated and scared. "But, yes, those are the details."

"Also, your school was threatened by the teachers union because of your staff's long hours and working conditions."

"Yes." Carl had never thought of the parallels between the working conditions in Booker T. Washington Charter Schools and Kiwi's Chinese operations.

"That's all for now." The FBI agent abruptly stood up, trying to contain his personal disdain for Carl and the things he represented— the harm caused to America by factories going overseas, Wall Street bankers, and anti-unionism. Tim came from a strong union family, with his father having worked in Detroit car plants. Towering over the principal, Tim said, "If you think of anything else, contact me. Here's my card. We'll be calling you back for another interview."

Chapter 3

The three Brightstone executives hunched over the African Black-wood table, reputedly the most expensive wood in the world, talking in hushed voices. The room was scanned daily for possible bugs. On the walls hung original paintings by Titian, van Gogh, Matisse, and a variety of modern works.

"That son-of-a-bitch out in Colorado, John Pillsbury, is giving us a hard time," said Jeremy King, vice-president of sales for the publishing and testing giant. Jeremy played a major role in making Brightstone a dominant player in the Common Core marketplace. He was tall, with his blond hair turning gray as he approached his fifties. Well dressed and groomed, his mannerisms often reminded people of a used-car salesman.

"We flew Pillsbury and his family to Jamaica, wining and dining them," Jeremy continued. "I slipped him some cash under the table, but Colorado still hasn't adopted our Common Core tests."

"Didn't we send him and other chief state school officers on a junket to Singapore?" John asked.

"This guy Pillsbury knows the Common Core will generate $35 billion a year in education business," answered Jeremy. "As state school head, he knows how much we'll make if Colorado adopts our tests and we can sell Common Core software to local schools. We're encountering similar problems with state school heads in North Carolina, Arizona, and Texas. Our biggest problems are in Massachusetts and California."

"What's the problem in those two states?" John grimaced at the thought of losing income from populated states.

"Strong anti-testing groups," Jeremy explained. "Some crazies and teachers are trying to convince the public that too much time is spent on testing. You always have crackpots like that whining about something."

"What's marketing got to say?" John punched a button on the table console, summoning an attendant. All attendants serving upper management were carefully screened and kept under constant surveillance by the firm's detective agency, Smott and Sons. They were required to sign a contract that forbad them from talking about company business.

John stood up, shedding the coat of his $50,000 Dormeuil suit, and handed it to the attendant who appeared at his side. John flew to the UK twice a year in the company's jet to ensure Dormeuil's tailors had his precise measurements. His sixty-year-old face looked forty and was creamy-smooth and free of blemishes from a yearly regime of cosmetic surgery. A combination of good tailoring and body sculpting gave his tall body an athletic appearance. A personal barber arrived every morning to shave, groom him, and ensure that no gray appeared in his raven-black hair.

"Anything else?" the uniformed attendant asked.

"Just hang it up, and bring more coffee," John snapped.

"We've got some big marketing problems," said Marty Cohn, vice-president of marketing, after John sat down. Short, pudgy, and always looking disheveled, Marty, because of his advertising genius, rose rapidly at Brightstone from assistant to being in charge of the marketing department.

"There are some holdouts among chief state school officers," Marty continued, "along with the fuss being caused by the anti-testing groups. And then there are the cheating scandals."

"Hell," John exclaimed, "I thought school people were supposed to be honest and moral! What's the story on the cheating?"

"The superintendent of Atlanta's schools was charged with racketeering. She received a $500,000 bonus for raising test scores and then was accused by the FBI of pressuring administrators and teachers to change student answer sheets. Stories of changed answer sheets are appearing all over the country." Marty paused to look at his list of issues on his Kiwi tablet. "A criminal ring was found in Southern states that sent substitutes to take the writing part of Brightstone's teacher performance test."

"They did what!" Jeremy exclaimed.

"They sold services over the Internet to candidates for state teaching certificates. The services included, for a fee of $5,000, a guarantee to pass the written exam by having a trained expert take it for them. It was reported that one substitute took the teacher exam five hundred times for other people," Marty explained.

"That's really something," said Jeremy, shaking his head. "What has this world come to, with cheating teachers and school administrators?"

"So, Marty, what's your plan to solve this mess?" John knew Marty had already devised some marketing strategies.

"There's another issue, which will explain my plan," Marty answered. "There are news reports from Illinois that students were throwing up and breaking down crying during Brightstone's tests."

Jeremy gasped. "Throwing up and crying! What's that all about?"

"The tests were all screwed up," Marty replied, indicating his displeasure with the situation. "Our testing department hired hotshot college professors, and I must say for a pretty penny, to put these tests together to meet Common Core requirements. Many questions were incomprehensible. I read some of them over and over again, and I couldn't make sense of them, particularly the essay parts.

"So the kids are told their whole future rides on their test scores, and they can't understand the questions," Jeremy observed. "No wonder they threw up. Probably thought they were on the school-to-prison pipeline if they failed. How the hell am I going to sell Brightstone's products, with this stuff going on?"

"Okay, Marty, give us the plan," John requested.

"First, we launch a public-relations campaign to protect our image." Marty suddenly stopped and asked, "Was this room checked for bugs this morning?"

"Yes, get to the plan," John ordered.

"We need to counter the images created by anti-testing groups, cheating scandals, and these crappy tests these hired dumbbells from the universities are creating."

"So, what's the PR campaign?" Jeremy asked.

"I'm proposing TV spots, billboards, and product placement in movies to create the image that Brightstone's tests are the best in the world and the key to career success."

"Product placement?" John repeated.

"We have a list of future movies that have something to do with schools. We'll pay to have scenes of smiling students taking Brightstone's tests. We're paying for one movie scene where a student leaving an exam room thanks Brightstone by name for a fair test that will guarantee her a job. That's all bullshit, of course, but it'll help our image."

"Anything in the plan to sell more tests?" Jeremy asked.

"We're hiring a bunch of education deans to appear on talk shows and write letters to newspapers, praising the Common Core and mandated tests. They will argue we need more testing to improve schools."

Jeremy chuckled at the self-serving nature of the strategy. "How much more testing will these paid-for education deans call for?"

"State mandated tests three times a year. We're hiring state lobbyists to see if we can get this requirement enacted in law. We could really multiple our earnings."

"Can we trust these education deans?" John asked.

"Servants of power and their pocketbooks—that's what many of these deans and professors are like. We do have to look out for the some of the wacko deans and professors who are campaigning against the Common Core and testing." Marty looked down at his Kiwi tablet to explain the next part of the strategy. "The PR campaign will create warm, positive feelings about testing. We're going to use preschool and kindergarten teachers and students. The public is frightened by pictures of teenagers. So we're showing happy and bright-eyed preschoolers and kindergarteners taking Brightstone's tests."

"What about the cheating scandals?" asked John, impatient to conclude the meeting, so he could hop on his helicopter and fly out for a round of golf.

"We're working with Kiwi on that—they're developing computer testing formats to guarantee security. Of course, we'll make more money, along with Kiwi, selling these systems to local schools."

"So we lobbied the feds and state governments"—Jeremy laughed—"to make mandated tests central to schooling and tied to teacher and principal bonuses. The result is an incentive for students, teachers, and school administrators to cheat. Then we sell them another product to fix something caused by the first product. This is a good sales strategy. Bravo!"

"Our problem is with Kiwi," Marty observed. "We have a close working relationship, supplying e-texts and linking testing programs to their tablets."

"What's wrong with Kiwi?" John asked.

"They've had riots at their Chinese plant. We've helped them with bribes to Communist Party officials, but now it's rumored to be a problem for the US FBI and Homeland Security."

"How'd they get involved?" John shouted, punching the attendant call button. The attendant quickly opened the door, and John yelled at her, "Call George and cancel my golf date."

"It's that charter-school bombing in Cincinnati and the secretary of education poisoning. The two appear linked in the investigation as terrorist acts. The principal of the bombed school is some former Wall Street hotshot turned do-gooder after making a fortune. He's heavily invested in the Common Core Fund, which Brightstone and Kiwi are dependent on for loans."

"Good Lord," Jeremy exclaimed. "Do you think they'll pull us into their investigative web?"

"They might when they find out, and I'm sure they will, that we helped bribe Chinese officials."

John punched the attendant button again. No phones were kept in the conference room because of possible bugs. John ordered the attendant to round up any members of Brightstone's legal team that might be in their offices and send them to the conference room.

"What about all those bribes we've been giving state officials and our lobbying efforts?" Jeremy felt a wave of panic at the idea of dealing with Homeland Security.

"Shit," Marty blurted out, "I hadn't thought of that, or I would have brought up the Kiwi issues at the beginning of our meeting."

"The only thing we can be sure of is that they haven't bugged any conversations in this room; at least, we hope." John dreaded the possibility of Homeland Security looking at Brightstone's record. "You know the National Security Agency has all our e-mails and phone calls stored in their data system. We can only hope they don't put the pieces together."

"What about this charter school in Cincinnati?" Jeremy asked Marty. "Besides the principal being invested in the Common Core Fund, is there a connection to us?"

"I saw a newspaper piece mentioning that a teacher confessed to changing test scores the day before the bombing. Ohio does use Brightstone tests, but it seems a little farfetched that they would use that to link us to the investigation."

"Shit, we did bribe the Ohio state head of education to get our tests adopted." Jeremy suddenly had a vision of being marched in handcuffs into a jail cell.

"Let's not panic until we talk to our lawyers." John tried to calm the other two. "This could be a problem. But we are in no way directly linked to the bombing or death. I don't think they'll look that closely at our National Security Agency data. A real problem might be our participating in bribing the Chinese."

"We did work closely with Secretary Blanchard to get the Department of Education to approve our tests," Marty explained. "We didn't bribe him. However, we did create the Brightstone Foundation, which awarded his daughter and son four-year scholarships to Harvard. I wonder if that will pop up in their data files. Those scholarships are worth a lot when you consider Harvard's tuition and room and board."

Chapter 4

"The FBI just called," Felicia Cochran, president of the Cincinnati Teachers Union, yelled across to the union's one employee, who sat hunched over her computer screen, trying to determine whether the union could continue to pay her salary.

"The FBI!" Joyce Murdoch, the union's executive secretary, exclaimed, looking across the sparsely furnished office. "What do they want?"

"Some agent will be here within the hour to talk about the bombing," Felicia answered. "We've got enough problems holding things together, without being dragged into that mess."

Both Felicia and Joyce were worried about the union's future. Criticisms of teachers unions were appearing daily in newspapers, and the 2010 movie *Waiting for Superman* had set the stage for blaming teacher unions for school failures. Felicia, an attractive and tall woman in her mid thirties, was elected to head the union on a platform of rebuilding the union's image and fighting for a better contract with higher wages. Divorced, she lived in a small apartment in Clifton, near the University of Cincinnati. Using little makeup, she tied her brunette hair back into a ponytail. She had grown bored after a decade of teaching high-school English and decided to do something new.

"We've got enough problems just trying to figure out how to pay our salaries," Joyce responded, "without the FBI. Does this mean hiring a lawyer?"

"I don't think that'll be necessary." Felicia looked over at Joyce, who was wearing clothes bought at a local thrift store. Unable to find a teaching job after graduating from Ohio State University, Joyce took the poorly paid union job, hoping it would give her contacts to get an elementary-school teaching position. In her early twenties, she lived with her born-again Christian parents, unable to afford her own apartment. She was cute, short, with curly blond hair, and her parents carefully monitored her social life while she dreamt of getting wild if she could earn enough to live independently.

"How does it look for the contract? Think I can get hired in the fall?" Joyce asked.

"I'm worried they're cutting jobs. We're fighting attempts to replace teachers with software and online instruction."

"Are they really trying to do that?"

"At the school board meeting last night, a sales rep from Kiwi technology was pushing their tablets. They claimed students wouldn't need much teaching supervision, using Kiwi software."

"Is that why I was required to take a course in educational technology? Are they really going to replace teachers with machines?"

"The school board announced they wouldn't be hiring anymore foreign-language teachers and will use online language instruction. The Kiwi sales rep presented studies showing online instruction was better than a teacher. I looked at the studies, and they were all statistical gobbledygook. They hire creeps from universities to do studies no one can understand."

"You think we'll strike?" asked Joyce, wondering if her chances of being a teacher were slipping away.

"Robots, that's what Kiwi wants. Teacher robots! Kiwi showed the school board plans for a math-teaching robot. Claims it will come complete with emotions. You know, smile at students and give them hugs."

"Hugs—I thought they were illegal." Joyce sat back in her chair and let her eyes wander from the computer screen to the large photo, hanging behind Felicia's head, of teachers-union hero Albert Shanker, leader of New York City's teachers union during the tumultuous '60s and '70s, who later became head of the national union. She wondered what he would do with teacher robots.

"Hugs from robots are okay, according to Kiwi. Since robots are not human, a machine hug works. No sexuality in the math-teaching robot's software. Kiwi claims great success with their robots in old-folk's homes. They kiss the elderly, with realistic-looking silicone lips."

"And if the robots get weird?"

Felicia smiled. "I saw a newspaper article about a robot going wild in an old-people's place in Japan. Suddenly they ran around hugging seniors, squeezing them in their mechanical arms. Six were hospitalized. Imagine if that happened in a classroom."

"How did the school board members react?" Joyce got up and refilled her cup at the small coffee machine on a corner table.

"A couple of technology buffs on the board liked the idea of robots. Some of the older, wealthy ones thought the idea strange. The digital freaks attacked them for being behind the times."

"Didn't mention I could be replaced by a robot when I took that technology course. The prof claimed technology would help me teach better, not replace me."

"I think the math-teacher robot is only the beginning." Felicia joined Joyce at the coffee machine. "Math is easy for programming a robot. Everything is pretty fixed in the Common Core math standards. But English and history may be problems if students ask the robot tricky questions. Robots can Google most questions, but they have a hard time dealing with ambiguity."

"Imagine a robot teaching Shakespeare or Mark Twain. I did hear there is software for grading essays." Joyce returned to her desk.

"The Kiwi sales rep Bob Carlson and I had drinks after the school-board meeting."

"And?" Joyce smiled, hoping this was the beginning of a love story.

"Bob said Kiwi is working with the Japanese to develop a literature-teaching robot that can change faces and voices. It can look like Mark Twain or Shakespeare and try to sound like them. I thought it was weird, since no one knows what Shakespeare sounded like."

"What'd he say to that?" Joyce was still hoping for a love story.

"It didn't matter. The robot will be linked to Kiwi's tablets and can stream reenactments of stories and plays. Students type in responses to questions based on the Common Core standards. The robot, he claimed, would scurry around the room, giving positive reinforcement with silicone kisses and hugs."

"Did you go with him after the drink?"

"Not my type. I think Bob probably uses robots to satisfy his needs. He even volunteered that the Japanese have some real neat love robots. No need to marry. I wondered, why bother having kids, when you could have robots that wouldn't whine or complain?"

"So there really isn't any hope for me getting a job?" Joyce sat down, looking forlorn, thinking about her wasted education, career plans, and student loans. She wondered if her born-again parents could handle her bringing a love robot into the house.

"What about me learning to take care of teaching robots?" Joyce asked. "That could be the future."

"Maybe Kiwi could train you. Bob said they're working on school-principal robots that would maintain the teaching robots—check them out for programming and mechanical problems."

"What? That sounds weird—robots checking robots. You mean they could also hug the teacher robots? How about principal and teacher robots having an affair? I guess that would be okay."

"I had a principal who tried to get me in bed; never worked. The robots will just share student test scores. If students are not learning the way they should, the principal robot would be alerted to the possible failure of the teaching robot and repair it or send it back to the factory."

"Are you serious?" Joyce exclaimed. "If this is true, I should jump on the bandwagon and be trained to care for robots."

"Kiwi Teacher Training School is being created at Horton University, you know, that elite school south of San Francisco, with a grant from the Brightstone Company: the company that makes tests and texts. Bob said it might be called the Brightstone-Kiwi Common Core Teacher Training School or something like that."

Felicia returned to her desk, feeling depressed by the news she was giving Joyce. She had not really thought through the implications of her conversation with Bob. You certainly couldn't unionize robots, she thought.

"You sure you and Bob didn't get a thing going?" Joyce asked hopefully, wanting to hear that someone had a love life.

"No, he's truly into robots. I got a little drunk from the free drinks at Kiwi's expense. I'm wondering what teacher robots will mean for our union. You should check out that Horton school; you might be the first in line for teacher-robot training. They call Horton the Ivy League school of California."

"Here it is." Joyce looked up from her computer screen. "He was close about the name. In a year it will open as the Horton University Brightstone-Kiwi School of Common Core Teacher Training and Robotics. It says here, 'Apply now for credentials in Teacher Robot Operations.' It claims that in three years robots will be replacing teachers around the country, with a guarantee of raising student test scores."

"Good God," Felicia responded. "I thought he was kidding about the robots taking over schools. Guarantees high test scores! Will you be credentialed?"

"They'll issue a credential for robotic teacher operations, and it claims that states are already putting into place a credentialing system for both robots and those charged with robot operations. They're offering full scholarships for the year the school opens. I'm applying."

Their conversation was interrupted when FBI agent Timothy Geary came walking through the door. Tim looked around at the photos of union leaders and the bare wood floors and window frames and at the two women. He stared for a minute at Felicia before asking, "Is this the teacher union office?"

"You must be the FBI guy who called." Felicia got up from her desk and offered her hand. "I'm Felicia Cochran, president of the Cincinnati Teachers Union, and this is Joyce Murdoch, our executive secretary. What can we do for you?"

"I just wanted to ask a few questions about the charter-school bombing." Tim seemed to want to hold on to Felicia's hand as he looked into her startlingly green eyes.

"What a tragedy! All those children—it made me sick. Now they're trying to arm teachers. You know some teacher might get crazy, carrying a gun." Felicia stared at Tim's scarred face and rough features.

"Did the union ever threaten the school?" Tim looked down at his note pad, afraid that he might be staring too intently at Felicia's face.

"We did picket the school when it opened. These charter schools are nonunion and threaten our existence."

"The principal, Carl Grinder, reported that someone tried to hit him with a sign and that his staff's cars were vandalized."

"I don't think anyone tried to hit him, and the cars were all parked on unsafe streets. I can't believe the anti-teachers-union movement has gotten this bad, trying to accuse us of bombing a school."

"Grinder said your union was the only group that ever threatened the school. He claimed you were conducting a national protest against Booker T. Washington Charter Schools. Is that right?"

Felicia gasped. "Surely you don't think the union bombed the school. Grinder's one of these fat-cat Wall Street types who think unions are causing poor kids to fail. They're a threat to us."

"Fat-cat Wall Street—what do you mean?" Tim looked up at Felicia.

"These rich kids from Ivy League schools thought they could save poor kids by working two years in public schools for Educators for the World. Most made a mess. Now, after making tons of money, they decide to be do-gooders. They blame unions for failing to teach kids. Then they start charters and campaign to keep us out."

"So charters are a threat to your union?"

"Yes and no. They are anti-union, but they're not as much of a threat as these tech companies, like Kiwi, trying to take over our jobs."

"Kiwi." Tim paused, thinking of Principal Grinder's involvement with Kiwi. "What do you know of them?"

"I talked to a sales rep last night. The latest thing is teacher robots. He thinks in five years teacher robots will take over our jobs. Of course, it would be difficult recruiting robots to the union."

"You're kidding," Tim responded, startled at the idea. "How could robots take over your jobs?"

"They're going to make the robots with friendly emotions and the ability to answer student questions. They'll talk through silicone lips—cheaper than regular teachers and you don't have to pay them benefits. It'll kill the unions."

"I can't imagine." Tim shook his head. He liked unions because of his dad's work in automobile factories. Like Felicia, he was repelled by Wall Street and anti-union types.

"How much contact have you had with Kiwi?" Tim asked.

"What's Kiwi got to do with us and the bombing?"

"Please answer the question."

"Besides a Kiwi phone, the only personal contact was last night, during and after the school-board meeting."

"That's when you talked to their sales rep?"

"Yes."

"In other words," Tim continued, "Booker T. Washington Charter Schools and Kiwi threaten the very existence of your union."

"Are you still suggesting that we had something to do with the bombing, and that somehow teachers unions are terrorist organizations?"

"I'm not suggesting anything." Tim was thinking about asking Felicia out for coffee or lunch after the interview. "This maybe a terrorist act—given the killing of the Secretary of Education—and Homeland Security wants to follow all leads. Have you had any contact with China?"

"China! What's China got to do with all this?

"Just tell me about any connection with China—you or your union."

"My only contact was a study trip two years ago with the Confucian Institute."

"What's the Confucian Institute?"

"When I got to Beijing, I found out that Confucian Institutes—they're all over the world—are part of the Chinese government's public-relations plan to sell Mandarin and positive views of China to the rest of the world. A professor on the trip called it cultural imperialism."

"How long were you there?"

"For the summer—about ten weeks."

"Did you have any contact with officials of the Chinese Communist Party?"

"Party officials were at every function, but I don't know how high up they were. I can't imagine they were that important, getting involved with a bunch of US teachers and college people."

"What about Kiwi?"

"You mean on the China trip? We did use Kiwi software as part of learning Mandarin. I remember that some important-looking guys from the party appeared to watch us use the software."

"Did you talk to any of them?"

"Are you kidding? I talked to the party representatives at Confucian Institute gatherings, but these other guys seemed unapproachable. The party people at the Institute looked as if gods entered the room when these officials arrived with escorts from the People's Liberation Army, and I thought at any moment they would kiss the big shots' feet."

"Did there appear to be any connection between these party officials and Kiwi?"

"Only that they were interested in the software. Some American—we were never introduced—sat with them. He could have been from Kiwi."

"Do you mind if I contact you later with any other questions?" Tim smiled at Felicia.

"No, I don't mind. But do you think there is some kind of connection between Kiwi and the Chinese Communist Party? Good God," Felicia blurted out. "Do you think there's a link between Kiwi's teacher robots and the Chinese Communist Party? Is this a plot to brainwash Americans?"

Chapter 5

They sat behind an ornate table, being served tea while looking through a one-way glass at a classroom of fifth-grade Chinese students being taught English by a robot dressed to look like a female American teacher. Li Luan, head of the Chinese Communist Party's Technology Planning Team (TPT), motioned to the smartly dressed attendant to refill his cup.

To Luan's right sat the president of Kiwi, Jack Phillipson, who had flown the day before from the San Jose airport, near company headquarters in Silicon Valley, to Beijing in Kiwi's corporate jet. Phillips made the trip frequently to visit their Beijing offices and their manufacturing plant in Jinan, a short distance from Beijing. He liked the long flight, because it gave him time to work out in the plane's small gym and receive a massage to the sound of soft music and calming aromatherapy. A quick shower, a meal, and a nap left him refreshed and ready to deal with Communist officials. The plane's crew consisted of a world-renowned chef, a masseuse, a physical therapist, a secretary, two personal servants, and a butler, along with the two experienced pilots.

To Luan's left sat Kiwi's vice-president for robotic teaching, Bert Robinson, who lived near the company's factory in Jinan. Bert had lived in China for five years while directing production of the Kiwi's new teaching robot. Despite his wife's complaints about dirty air and contaminated food, he liked China. But he had to agree with his wife that air quality in Jinan might be shortening their lives. Bobby, their seven-year-old son, developed respiratory problems from the polluted air and was sent back three months ago to live with his grandparents. Jennifer, Bert's wife, who worked for Kiwi as vice-president of the Department of Robotic Emotions, remained in China, missing her son.

Seated behind Luan were an interpreter and several staff members from the party's TPT. Having studied at MIT, Luan's English was very good. He relied on the interpreter when he didn't completely understand what was being said.

On the other side of the one-way window, a robot rolled between the aisles of twenty-five fifth-graders, smiling with realistic silicone lips and nodding approval as students worked on English composition, typing on the screens of their Kiwi tablets.

"The writing is immediately communicated to the robot, who we're calling Sally, and assessed using Kiwi software. The essay-correcting software was tested in California schools and found to be as reliable as an average human English teacher."

"We did have that one problem." Jack reminded Bert, not wanting the Chinese to think they were hiding anything.

Turning to Luan, Jack explained. "The software couldn't distinguish between words that could be used as verbs, nouns, and adjectives, like the word 'run.' But we called in our team from Horton University's English department. I think most of the English professors are on our payroll. Always good to work with the West Coast's top school, and we can use their testimonials for marketing."

"Good idea." Luan nodded. "Everyone wants to hear from top schools, particularly in China, where students struggle to get into a school like Horton. Maybe they'll think that being taught by a Sally will get them into a good American school."

They watched Sally roll to the front of the class and begin speaking in English. "Good work, students. Today you learned to write sentences.

Next we will learn to speak." Pointing at a small, uniformed girl sitting in the second seat of the first row, Sally commanded, "Chu, read your essay to the class."

"We've got to do something about Sally's voice," Jack said to Bert. "She sounds too harsh. We should get the voice of someone like Meryl Streep or Julia Roberts. Also, a big-name actress would help marketing."

Bert dutifully typed the request into his tablet. "What about her dress? Jennifer was concerned that Sally's clothes were not helping with her showing positive emotions."

"I can see what she means." Jack looked thoughtfully through the class, as Sally rolled over and gave Chu a gentle hug and kiss. The student looked disgusted when Sally's silicon lips touched her cheek.

"We've got to cut out the kissing. It may be okay, since it's a robot, but I can imagine how it feels," Jack observed. "And get some designers from Ralph Lauren to work on clothing that gives a warm charm to Sally. What do you think, Luan? Should we use a Chinese designer for the China market?"

"Ralph Lauren is very popular in China," Luan answered, taking a sip of his tea. "My golf outfits come from his Beijing store. Lauren should work. I could probably cut a deal to get the teacher's dresses made here. We're going to need plenty if we get a global market for these robots."

Luan sat back, thinking about contacting his cousin Wang Bing to have robot clothes made in Bing's factory in Guangzhou. Bing, of course, would give Luan some of the profits, who would pass a percentage on to party officials.

"We might want designers from regional areas. I'm not sure Qatar or Saudi Arabia is going to want Ralph Lauren robots," Jack suggested. "We could use robots with hijabs or even burkas."

"You think Muslim dress codes will apply to robots?" Luan laughed. "They're not human. We could try a faceless robot with our Muslim populations. Many of our ethnic groups want to protect their dress. I'm wondering about robot Tibetan teachers."

"I think a burka might interfere with Sally's ability to guide her motion," Bert warned.

At that moment, Chang Bao, a little girl sitting at the end of the third row who had not been feeling well, sprayed her lunch of partially digested noodles and chicken onto the floor. Some of the vomit splattered on students sitting next to her, causing them to jump up, holding their hands over the mouths and noses while making gagging sounds.

Sally sensed and heard the students' movements. "Please be seated, or receive a demerit. You should not leave your desk until I tell you to."

The robot started rolling down the aisle as Bao let lose another geyser, leaving nearby students with stringy noodles clinging to their clothes. Some students retched and ran to the classroom's door.

"Stay calm, and carry on," Sally ordered, as her robotic wheels spun her in circles in the middle of the aisle, knocking over student desks. "Stay calm and carry on," Sally's mechanical voice began to repeat, as her wheels rolled through Bao's lunch and spread trails of yellow vomit around the room.

Embarrassed, Chang Bao tried to hide from Sally's optical sensors in a classroom corner.

Sally's software identified Bao as the problem and promptly sent the robot rolling toward the child, leaving a trail of yellow smashed chicken and noodles. As Sally called out, "Stay calm, and carry on," Bao ran to an adjacent corner.

The robot whirled around, following Bao and then slipping on the remains of the lunch. It hit two students and knocked them into the yellow slime.

Sally lay on its back, with its rollers spinning and its steady sounding voice calling out, "Stay calm, and carry on." Its robots arms began banging on the floor, spreading more of Bao's lunch.

Bert punched a command on his tablet, shutting down Sally's operation.

"What happened?" Luan yelled out angrily. "I thought this robot was ready to go. Our TPT office is set to begin marketing."

Jack looked at Bert. "I'm sure this can be easily corrected. What do you think, Bert?"

Bert looked sadly down at his tablet and began to stroke the Kiwi logo of the world shaped like a kiwi fruit. "I don't think anyone thought of how a teacher robot would handle a kid vomiting. We worked into the software protection against shooters, with the robot's communication system immediately contacting the police and attacking and disarming the gunman while telling students to stay calm and carry on. We've tried this in our lab, and it functioned okay. But no one thought about illness."

"Sally didn't seem very sympathetic about the student's vomiting." Jack stared at the confusion in the classroom, as teacher helpers rushed in to clean the floor and students. Bao sat hunched over in her corner, crying. "What's this about 'staying calm and carrying on'?"

"Sally's programmed to react to any unexpected student movements, particularly multiple student movements, by telling students to stay calm. The assumption is that any confused movements involving several students are either fights or an outsider entering the room. There is nothing in the software to deal with student vomit," Bert replied.

"What about sympathy and empathy? Are those emotions in Sally?" Jack realized that this flawed demonstration might hold up production for months. Kiwi had agreed to Luan's demand that the Communist Party's TPT would be compensated in cash for any delays.

"The Department of Robotic Emotions has worked on the programming problems related to sympathy and empathy. Jennifer claims basic human emotions are too difficult to program. Her department worried that including these emotions would cause Sally to become like a Jainist, afraid that any motion might harm or kill something, even a small insect. Trying to program Sally for empathy toward humans is still being worked on. Otherwise, empathy for all living things causes Sally's motherboard to burn up, as it reacts to multiple inputs and commands. A fly in the classroom might cause an empathetic Sally to shut down."

"So you're telling me," Luan said, "that Sally can't deal with classroom problems like a student's illness or even an accidental injury."

"Do you have kids?" Luan glared at Bert.

"Yes, and I know what you're going to say next. Kids get sick and hurt," Bert replied.

"What can you do?" Jack asked. "We have a lot of money riding on this robot. Booker T. Washington Charter Schools just put in a big order. They want all their charter schools operated by robots. Brightstone is counting on linking their testing to these robots."

"We've thought of putting in a panic button when the robot senses confusion in the classroom. The panic button would call the person in charge of school robotic operations. Of course, since it is planned that a school would have only one person for robotic operations, this would be a problem if several teacher robots activated their panic buttons at the same time."

"How long do you think it will take to straighten out this problem?" Jack asked, now worried about the reaction of party officials. Kiwi had already received help from the party to deal with the suicides and riots. But Communist Party leaders such as Luan might not continue to help. A delay in production of the teacher robots would reduce the flow of income into party coffers.

"Well, Luan, it looks like a minor delay in production," Jack said.

"Not a minor delay if we're dealing with emotions," Luan responded. "When we worked on robots at MIT, this was always a problem. I don't think other government officials are going to be happy keeping troops at your factory with no payoff."

"We should talk in private." Jack stood up. "Can everyone clear the room?" He waved at Bert and the retinue from the TPT to leave.

Luan nodded at his staff and waited until they were alone before saying, "Jack, this delay will cause problems. It's not cheap to keep the People's Army at your Jinan plant."

"Kiwi will draft a check for your consulting work today," Jack responded. "It will be large enough to cover whatever money you need to spread around until production actually starts."

"Empathy!" Bert's wife Jennifer exclaimed when he returned to Jinan the next day. "We can't program robots for empathy or sympathy. If we could, I don't know what the consequences might be."

"What consequences?" Bert asked, looking out from their twelfth-floor apartment, unable to see the street below through the thick smog.

"Can you imagine a world where robots have empathy? Do unto others as you would have them do onto you is the basic framework of empathetic thinking. This would require robots to feel or imagine the emotions of others."

"I still don't quite understand." Bert shook his head and commented, "I think the air is getting worse. We might want to get back to the States soon."

"If robots could feel the emotions of humans, would they also be able to feel the emotions of other robots? Empathy is key to human social relations," Jennifer continued. "If robots could have empathetic feelings toward other robots, then they could have social relationships."

"You mean robots could become friends with each other?"

"Look, I don't think we can program robots for empathy, but if we could, then it would be possible for robots to develop social relations with each other." Jennifer came over to the window to look at the morning smog, thinking of her son back in the States.

"That could defeat the idea of teacher robots," Bert replied.

"Why?"

"One reason for developing teacher robots, as I understand, is to have compliant workers who don't form unions," Burt answered. "Empathy could result in teacher robots uniting to help each other."

"A teacher robot union is a wild idea," replied Jennifer.

"So you're saying you cannot program teacher robots for feeling sympathy or empathy toward students."

"That's right! The Department of Robotic Emotions is not that advanced, to program those emotions. But so what? I don't think any of my teachers ever felt sympathetic toward me. It might be better to have teachers that were without empathy."

"It didn't work yesterday when the kid threw up. Classroom chaos is what I witnessed."

"We'll have to put a panic button in the robot program. The robot can activate it if students get out of control," Jennifer observed.

"I wonder if the Booker T. Washington Charter Schools are going to care if robots feel sympathy toward their students." Maybe sympathy and empathy get in the way of good teaching, Bert thought.

"Knowing Brightstone and Kiwi and the people in the US Department of Education," Jennifer observed, "I think they want to get all emotions out of teaching. Do test prep, and then assess. Isn't that the new education standard? Our teacher robots can do that."

Chapter 6

"What, the robot failed!" Mary Phillipson, president of the Phillipson Foundation, yelled into the phone to her husband in China. "What are we to do about Brightstone and the Booker T. Washington Charter Schools?"

"We'll have to work something out when I get back," Jack Phillipson replied, sitting on the couch in his suite at the Raffles Hotel, near Beijing's Tiananmen Square. "Right now I'm concerned about Li Luan and his friends. This is going to slow production. They're pretty upset after all our promises and my convincing them they should use the army at the Jinan plant."

"How much?" Mary asked, knowing bribes would have to be paid.

"You should wire Luan $100,000 and put it down as consulting work for research studies on teaching robots. He'll spread the money around to his friends."

Looking at the broad expanse of the Pacific from her office window in the three-story, all-glass building perched on a cliff just north of Santa Cruz, Mary began to sort out the problems caused by the teaching-robot failure. The poisoning of Secretary Blanchard had left the foundation and Kiwi without a major supporter in Washington. Secretary Blanchard had hired a number of the Phillipson

Foundation's staff to fill vacancies in the Department of Education's Office of Innovation. These former staff members remained loyal to the foundation and advocated for teaching-robots in every classroom.

"Get me either Marvin Goldman or Abe Stein," Mary ordered through the intercom. This is going to be a blow to their plans, Mary thought. The grants to the Booker T. Washington Charter Schools were the only thing keeping them going. Marvin and Abe were planning to reduce staff costs with teacher robots. She knew the two were channeling charter-school money into a private investment fund to which she and her husband, along with Brightstone's President John Greenwood, belonged. They'd all laughed over lunch at San Francisco's Union Club when they called it the Common Core Fund. The fund's investment goal was to control the for-profit education market. Currently, the fund was loaning money to Brightstone and Kiwi to keep them afloat.

"Marvin, the teaching-robot failed. From what Jack said, it couldn't handle a student medical problem. The head of robotic teaching doesn't know how long it will take to fix the program."

"There's no timeline? We need the teaching robots by next fall, or there will be problems for the Common Core Fund and our charters," Marvin replied, on the other end of the line.

"I know," Mary responded. "The problem is complicated by Blanchard's poisoning. He was going to help with a public announcement about the robots. We don't know what will happen without federal support."

"Can we find someone else in the Department of Education to serve on the board of the Common Core Fund?" Marvin asked.

"Remember, the deal with Blanchard was that he would serve and then become head of the fund when he left the government. I don't know of anyone else we could trust."

"What about the foundation people you got Blanchard to hire? Could we use any of them? We will all be in a mess over this delay." Marvin was sounding desperate.

"The only one might be Jean Nolan," Mary replied. "We got Blanchard to appoint her head of the Office of Innovations. We gave

Jean some stock in Kiwi. She's doing a good job promoting teacher robots. I don't know how she'd do heading an investment fund."

"We don't have to make the same promises as we had to with Blanchard—maybe give Jean some more Kiwi stock to promote the teacher robots. When will you see her?"

"She'll be out here tomorrow. Jean spends half her time at the foundation and the other half in Washington. Blanchard agreed to that arrangement. I don't know if a new secretary would."

"Do you think the three of us could talk tomorrow? Are your conference lines secured from the National Security Agency taps?"

"We should be okay with a secure conference call. This call is secure. We have Kiwi technicians in daily to make sure the agency can't record important messages. I know Brightstone holds their meetings in a secure room. They don't trust anything, including Kiwi technicians."

"Abe and I will fly out tomorrow to meet with you. I'm going to contact John Greenwood to see if he can meet. There's too much at stake with the bombing in Cincinnati and its ties to our investment fund."

Mary hung up and noticed a warning light flashing on her console. Oh, shit, she thought, I wonder if that was recorded. "David," she called her security office, "I see the warning light is flashing. What's up?"

"We just detected a probe from a Chinese server. Do you know of any reason for the Chinese hacking our communications?"

"There could be some problems with China. What do you advise? Do you think they recorded my last phone call?"

"Why don't we meet in our secure room?"

"Okay," Mary answered. She got up and started walking to the Phillipson Foundations' secure room, next to her office, wondering what agency in the China was trying to hack their systems. She'd heard that the Chinese government was investigating corruption and bribes from foreign companies.

She entered the secure room, where security people were again checking for bugs. David Smyth, head of Kiwi and the Phillipson

Foundations' security team, entered and sat down across from Mary at the room's conference table. They both remained silent, until the other security people left the room.

"So what issues might we have with China?" David asked. "Their hackers are really good. We need to know the source of the problem. Is it the government or a private person?"

"We've been bribing one government official, Li Luan, head of the Chinese Communist Party's Technology Planning Team, whose been passing on parts of the bribe to others. Some is going to army generals to protect Kiwi's Jinan plant. The robot failed, and Luan is pretty upset. We're giving him more money through the foundation. So it could be him or his associates."

"Any other possibilities?" David made a written note to see if his security team could hack into Luan's messages and accounts. David used only written materials. He never used a tablet or computer to store notes and had only paper files, knowing the cyber-spying ability of the government.

"There's a government corruption probe—it's a big thing in China, with all the complaints about graft." Mary paused, trying to think of any other potential hackers. "It could be a private citizen or an unhappy worker at the Jinan plant."

"Yesterday we experienced a number of Chinese probes into Kiwi's system. We blocked them. They may be related to the teaching robot."

"Tomorrow, we're having a meeting to discuss the robot issue. Jack is still in China. Do we dare try an online or video conference?"

"God, no, the Chinese access all communications going out of the country. You'll be heard for sure. In fact, I'd take a walk through Wilder Park and find a tree to sit under. I won't trust anyplace, given the cyber-spying by the Chinese and our government."

So the next day, Mary, Jean Nolan and Marvin Goldman along with Abe Stein from the Booker T. Washington Charter Schools, Brightstone's Vice President of Marketing Marty Cohn, Brightstone Foundation's head Rueben Bush, and Kiwi's Vice President of School Technologies Gordon Brader followed a trail through the Wilder

Ranch State Park, looking for a comfortable place to have their secret meeting.

"Over there." Mary pointed at a spot on a hill. "We should be safe. I've got some towels, for sitting, in my backpack. David checked the backpack for any bugs."

"I don't think you have to worry about the Feds backing off support of teacher robots, unless the president appoints someone who is opposed," Jean Nolan said, almost whispering, after the group had sat down in a small circle. "Who could object to teacher robots? They're so much better than regular teachers."

"The Brightstone Foundation," Rueben Bush informed them, "has been in touch with its congressional representatives to ensure a new secretary who is friendly to us and the robot project. We're still funding anti-teacher and anti-union groups. Polls show that the public is swinging away from supporting live teachers to wanting robot teachers."

"Our investors will be nervous if they hear about the China problem," Marvin Goldman explained. "Any major withdrawals from the Common Core Fund could mean trouble for us."

"Hollywood is releasing *Super Teacher* next week," Mary said. "It was supposed to become public at the same time as the announcement of the success of Kiwi's teacher robot. The Phillipson Foundation spent a lot funding the movie—Arnold Schwarzenegger was to play the teacher robot but cancelled before it went into production. We got the California Teacher of the Year to play the part, with a testimonial at the end on the superiority of teacher robots."

"It should help, even with the delay," Rueben commented. "Our foundation's support of anti-teacher media worked. The polls show public anger at teachers increasing after we plastered the country with billboards and television spots showing crying students pleading for good teachers. With *Super Teacher*, we are launching another set of public ads showing students hugging their teacher robots."

"Let's get to the real problem." Abe Stein leaned forward and spoke in a hushed voice. "If there are significant withdrawals from the Common Core Fund, we cannot cover them all. A lot of money was channeled from the fund to the Phillipson Foundation to bribe Chinese officials and to support US political candidates. It cost us a pretty penny to get Blanchard appointed as secretary of education. I don't know if we have enough to get another friend in the Department of Education."

"There are also the fund's bonuses we've been paying each other," Marvin reminded the group. "We've been getting rich over all this anti-teacher and pro-technology stuff."

"We also must worry about the Chinese invested in the fund. I don't know what might happen if the Chinese army investors lose their shirts," Mary warned. "I wonder if they'll take it out on us."

"Jesus," Marty exclaimed, "do you think the Chinese are involved in poisoning Blanchard?"

Mary reminded the group, "We convinced a number of US senators and congresspeople to invest in Brightstone and Kiwi. Of course, they backed bills funding educational technology. They're going to be pissed if their investments fail."

"What do you think we should do?" Jean asked the group. "I could get someone in the Department of Education to make a public statement about the importance of teaching robots."

"That's a good idea," Marty said. "Brightstone could do a press release congratulating Kiwi for its successful robot and mentioning that it's undergoing fine-tuning."

"Kiwi and the Phillipson Foundation could do the same thing," Mary declared. "Make it sound like everything is coming along smoothly. We're giving Luan some consulting money, and we should be able to convince him to do the same thing in the Chinese press."

"Let's hope this works, for now." Abe shook his head, thinking about the consequences and possible jail terms for all of them. "But we must get a working robot into America's classroom. Without a teaching robot, we're screwed."

"I won't know exactly the timeline for the robot until Jack returns. Our security expert David Smyth says we shouldn't have any communications with China because of their hackers and ours." Mary stood up with the group, and they walked back to the trail and out of the park.

No one in the group noticed the camouflaged figure hunkered down in the bushes on an opposite hill, using a long-range laser microphone to record their conversation.

Chapter 7

Entering the Houston charter school headquarters, Agent Tim Geary was greeted by a life-size statue of Booker T. Washington with words inscribed on its base: "If you can't read, it's going to be hard to realize dreams." Other quotes from Washington were carved into the wall behind the receptionist's desk. A blue flag hung from the ceiling, proclaiming, "Few things can help an individual more than to place responsibility on him, and to let him know that you trust him."

"I called earlier about interviewing Marvin Goldman and Abe Stein," Agent Geary told the receptionist. "I'm FBI Agent Tim Geary."

"They're expecting you on the third floor," replied Kim Luke, who was distracted by the Angry Bird game she was playing on her phone and waved a hand at a bank of elevators. "When you get out, follow the yellow line marked 'Path to Success.' It will take you to a door marked 'Test for the Best.' That's the conference room."

Putting her phone down, she looked at the FBI agent. "I know it sounds weird. But the building was paid for by Brightstone, which insists we give testing a positive spin. The last Brightstone person to visit told me to play Angry Birds to help me pass the Brightstone test for the local community college."

Above the elevators, Tim read the sign "Up from Slavery: Success is to be measured not so much by the position that one has reached in life as by the obstacles which he has overcome."

The elevator doors were embossed with likenesses of Booker T. Washington and his words, "If you want to lift yourself up, lift up someone else," along with Brightstone logos proclaiming, "Brightstone tests will lift you to success."

Stepping onto the third floor, Tim immediately saw the yellow line running along a well-lit hallway with walls covered with slogans such as "Learning is Power; Testing gives you Power," and "The road to success is paved with Brightstone Tests."

One sign caused Tim to stop and stare as he made his way down the Path to Success. "Teacher Robots: Our Hope, Our Future."

The day before, Tim had met with Alan Olsen, secretary of the Department of Homeland Security, in Washington. The bomb squad had reported that the school explosion was caused by a small amount of C-4 explosive placed somewhere in the school's storage room. Alan gave his data specialists the task of finding sources for the bomb material. Alan asked Tim to list the potential suspects. When Tim mentioned Li Luan, Alan exclaimed, "Holy shit, you mean the Chinese Communist Party might be involved?"

Ricin, another investigative team found, got into US Secretary of Education Paul Blanchard's system through the contents of a large envelope handed to Blanchard by an aide on the morning of his death. The aide told investigators someone handed him the envelope, saying it was from the president's office. The envelope was marked with what looked like official stickers and stamps. A message on the outside read, "For Secretary Paul Blanchard's Eyes Only." Not suspecting the envelope contained poison, the aide dutifully passed it on to the secretary. The opened envelope was found in the secretary's room with what was identified as a ricin substance coating the inside. Investigators could not find any fingerprints, other than the aide's and the secretary's. The manila envelope could be purchased in any stationery store. Investigators were examining the stickers and stamps for any clues.

Teacher robots came up when Frank Sawhill, a National Security Agency big-data analyst, informed them that Brightstone, Kiwi, the Booker T. Washington charters, and their foundations were all linked in a web to an investment account called the Common Core Fund. "Every time we looked at the e-mails about the fund, there was something about teacher robots." Sawhill informed them. "However, they seem to have developed some sophisticated systems to block our spyware. We couldn't find out much more about the teacher robots. We also noted that some Chinese servers were trying to gain access to the Common Core Fund. This is causing some real problems for our analysis. The worst would be if they kept paper files and only sent things in handwritten notes.

Marvin Goldman and Abe Stein were already sitting at the rough-hewn wooden conference table when Agent Geary entered through the door marked "Test for the Best."

"We got the table from Washington's old house," the Marvin informed Tim, seeing him eye the unpainted table. "We think it's inspirational. It reminds us that our kids can make it to the top. Maybe, like Washington, they can have dinner with the president if they test well in school."

Tim sat down and pulled out his coat pocket his notebook of questions. "I thought Booker T. Washington had something to do with slavery. What's he got to do with your kids?"

"Well, our kids were slaves in public schools," Abe answered. "Most are poor and black, though we're recruiting more Latinos. Using Washington's methods, we'll free them to rise to the top."

"I noticed a sign in the hall about teacher robots. What's that got to do Washington's methods?"

"Most of the teachers in this country are white," Marvin replied, checking his Kiwi tablet for text messages. "White teachers oppress black students. We think public schools operate like slave plantations, with their rules and punishments. Teacher robots will overthrow white school oppression. Robots are color-blind."

"Up from public-school slavery," Abe interjected, "is our hope for kids in our charter schools.

Tim opened his notebook, trying to digest the idea of robots freeing students from public-school slavery.

"Do you know of anyone who might want to bomb your charter school in Cincinnati?" was Tim's first question.

"We can't think of anyone," Marvin answered. "You can imagine our discussions about the bombing. We wracked our brains and couldn't think of a person or group that would want to do us harm."

"Your Principal Grinder mentioned the teachers union. Any thoughts on that?"

"Can't imagine," Abe answered. "We thought of the teachers union as a possibility, but we don't think they would go that far. They may be slave drivers and try to whip these kids into failure, but I don't think they're violent."

"They're wage slaves," Marvin added. "Those union creeps think only about money and their salaries. Public schools are just schools of slavery for students and teachers."

"Hm," Tim looked down thoughtfully at his notes, distracted by thoughts of Felicia whenever unions were mentioned. "What about your connections with Brightstone? I noticed their name on the elevator door."

"They paid for the building," Abe answered. "We couldn't survive without funding from the Brightstone Foundation and, of course, the Phillipson Foundation."

"You also get federal money?"

"Yes, we've received federal grants to support our Booker T. Washington weekend and summer camps. I don't know what will happen with Blanchard dead. He was a great supporter of our schools."

"What about your work with Brightstone? Why are they pouring so much money into your charter schools?"

"Frankly," Abe said, "they agree with us that public schools are slave plantations for whipping people into shape. They've helped with materials to launch our freedom curriculum based on common core standards."

"Freedom curriculum." Tim shook his head, feeling uneasy about interviewing anti-unionists. "What does that mean? And what has Brightstone done?"

"Freedom and equality are the foundation ideas of our charters," Marvin answered, looking up at a large portrait of Booker T. Washington on the wall. "Washington said, 'I had the feeling that to get into a schoolhouse and study would be about the same as getting into paradise.' Charter schools are paradise for our students."

"Let me explain," Abe interrupted. "Sometimes these students get confused about freedom and equality. They think equality will lead to freedom. We teach that equality leads to slavery."

"I don't understand." Tim shook his head, wondering where the discussion would lead.

"Washington understood that equality was not the answer," Marvin replied. "He said, if I may quote—and I should mention all our students must memorize Washington's famous statement—'The wisest among my race understand that agitations of social equality is the extremist folly, and that progress in the enjoyment of all privileges that will come to us must be the result of severe and constant struggle rather than of artificial forcing.'"

"What's that got to do with freedom and Brightstone?"

"We teach those kids that social equality isn't possible, but they can get rich by working hard. We make them memorize another Washington saying: 'Among a large class, there seemed to be a dependence upon the government for every conceivable thing. The members of this class had little ambition to create a position for themselves, but wanted the federal officials to create one for them.' Our curriculum repeats this message: 'Freedom is not depending on government but on yourself.'"

"This is basic to the Common Core Standards," Abe added. "Don't agitate for equality and be free from government dependency. That's what we're all about. Close the slave plantation called public schools."

"Brightstone helped us create a curriculum and tests based on Washington's ideas about equality and freedom. Then Kiwi helped us with a specially designed tablet."

"So you've worked with Kiwi also?" Tim made a note to call Felicia when he got back. She'd cry, he thought, if he told her about the comparison of public schools with slave plantations.

"Kiwi made a computer tablet shaped like Booker T. Washington's head, with a screen looking like his face," Marvin explained. "Around the edges of the head are buttons students push to hear quotes from his book *Up From Slavery*."

"Quotes like the ones you've been citing?" asked Tim.

"The computer tracks student work, and, if students seem to be drifting away from freedom to wanting government dependency, they are given a mild electrical shock. If they seem to want equality, they are given a stronger shock."

"Yes," Abe added gleefully, "if their thinking drifts to freedom and working hard, the tablet dispenses candy right out of Washington's mouth on the tablet's bottom."

"I saw something about teacher robots in the hallway. Are you working with Kiwi on that?" Tim asked.

"Of course," Marvin and Alan said in unison. "A teaching robot is Booker T. Washington's dream. It will end the slave mentality of public schools. It eliminates teachers as wage slaves and gives students the freedom to work at their own pace, without the involvement of government."

"With built-in assessments," Alan added, "the robot will be able to determine if the student's mind is drifting towards slavery—meaning wanting big government."

"Does the robot then shock the student if they think of more Social Security?" Tim smiled at his own question.

"No, our robot is being programmed for emotions, unlike the computer tablet. It will frown, smile, and hug, depending on where the student's mind is drifting. More freedom and less equality get a big hug."

"When will you get the robots?" Tim asked. "I understand Kiwi is having some problems."

"How did you find that out?" Marvin blurted out. They had all agreed at the meeting in Wilder Ranch Park not to mention the robot problem.

"NSA, the National Security Agency, helps us keep track of things. Do you think the Chinese Communist Party might use these robots to promote a love of China and communism?"

"God, no," Marvin answered. "Brightstone and Kiwi promise us robots that will free students to think of the greatness of free markets and limited government. Communism is about equality. Booker T. Washington schools are about freedom to work hard and accepting that the rich are rich because they worked hard."

"Sometimes we joke," Abe added, "that the Tea Party will be overwhelmed with our graduates. I know Booker T. would have loved Tea Party Republicans."

Chapter 8

"Hi, Felicia, Tim Geary here; how are you doing?"

"I don't know if this is a pleasant or worrisome surprise, hearing from you," Felicia Cochran answered from her desk in the teachers union's office. "You got more questions? Have you got the bad guys?"

"I'm not calling about the investigation. I'll be in Cincinnati tomorrow, and I was wondering if we could meet for dinner or drinks tomorrow night."

"Well, that is interesting." Felicia smiled. She had been thinking about him since their first meeting. "You're not going to play big FBI agent with me? You know—cross-examine me about my life?"

"Social," Timothy replied, happy to hear her interest. "I could meet you at your office. When do you finish work?"

"Five would be fine. So, how are things going?"

"Honestly, Felicia, Homeland Security ordered us not to spend time on phones because of cyber-spying. I'll explain when I see you at your office tomorrow at five."

Tim hung up the public phone inside the terminal at Houston's George Bush International Airport as the boarding announcement was made for his flight to Cincinnati.

Arriving at the Cincinnati/Kentucky airport in the early afternoon, Tim walked through an almost-empty terminal. After Delta stopped using the airport as a hub, some terminals shut, and many businesses closed. The airport was like a ghost town.

Locating his car in the long-term parking lot, Tim drove from the airport's Kentucky location to the downtown offices of Frank Bollinger, republican congressman from Ohio's Second Congressional district. Secretary of Homeland Security Alan Olsen had ordered him to visit the congressman after talking to the founders of the Booker T. Washington Charter Schools.

"Bollinger called me and wanted to be interviewed about the secretary's poisoning. They were close friends," Olsen told Tim. "He's chair of the House Committee on Education and the Workforce and, according to our data, is linked to the Common Core Fund, Brightstone, and Kiwi. See him when you get back to Cincinnati."

Tim parked his car near the federal building and headed to his 3:00 p.m. appointment with Bollinger. He was quickly ushered into Bollinger's office, which indicated to him that Bollinger gave the meeting high priority.

Sitting at a large mahogany desk flanked by Ohio and American flags, Bollinger was a medium-sized man in his fifties with balding gray hair. Dressed in a dark suit, his coat lapel sported US flag and Don't Tread on Me pins.

"It's such a tragedy." Bollinger waved Tim into a chair in front of his desk. "Secretary Blanchard was a dear friend and knew what would help our schools. I can't imagine who would kill him. Are there any clues?"

"We can't talk about the investigation at this point." Tim sat down, taking out his notepad. He was a little nervous talking to a congressman and wanted to follow the rules. "The head of Homeland Security said you wanted to be interviewed about the case."

"They're a lot of crackpots out there sending me daily e-mails about the schools. Some of them sound threatening. I'll turn all of them over to you for the investigation. I bet one of these crazy groups might have done it and maybe even the bombing."

"What kind of groups?"

"Well, there are these nutcases in Family Planning for America and Giving Women a Choice."

"I thought they were concerned with abortion?" Tim scribbled the two organization names on his note pad.

"They've got their fingers in everything; you know these crazy left-wing types." Bollinger picked up a flyer lying on his desk. "See this!" Bollinger pointed at a caricature of himself next to a picture of a condom with an X through it. "Imagine them passing out something with me next to a rubber. They just want to kill the unborn."

"I don't understand. How is this related to the poisoning?"

"Secretary Blanchard and our committee were working closely on a national abstinence education program for schools. The only sure way of not getting pregnant or AIDS is not doing it. It's also the only godly approach to sex education."

"So you think there's a possibility these two groups could have poisoned him, because they objected to your abstinence education program."

"First, they objected to our federally funded posters like the one saying 'Pet Your Dog and Not Your Date.' Then they made fun of us by issuing their own posters."

"How is that a problem?" Tim asked.

"The posters they're passing around criticize Secretary Blanchard and contain such weird things as 'Killer condoms stalk the night in search of teens who break purity pledges.'" Bollinger picked up a poster showing a toothy demon figure in a school hallway.

"You think this might be a sign they'd kill the secretary?" Tim stared at the poster, wondering if Bollinger was putting him on.

"You can see they're trying to undermine our campaign. Look at this T-shirt." Bollinger held up a T-shirt showing a hand with wedding rings on each finger and the message, "Keep your hands to yourself in style! Silver 'Savin' It' rings emit purity-packed Virgin-O rays proven to kill all crabs, gay germs, and hormone-producing sex glands!"

"Or take this one." Bollinger held up another T-shirt that said, "Your virginity is a precious golden butterfly to be purchased from your father by your future husband!"

"Can you imagine? They're attacking our program by saying we favor buying brides. My local church is trying to stop these attacks," the congressman continued, "with T-shirts proclaiming, 'Gay and straight teens alike can avoid eternal hellfire by saving sex for man-woman marriage' or this one from the Mississippi's 'Just Wait' program: 'Real Love Waits for Marriage.' The one I really like shows a padlock on a teenage boy's pants zipper with 'Just Say No' written on his pants. If they'd keep it zipped up, we won't have so many unwanted children. There would be no reason for abortion."

"We'll look into these groups," Tim responded, wondering why his boss sent him to listen to this stuff. "Are there any other groups you suspect of the poisoning?"

"We've had a lot of problems with the evolution curriculum." Bollinger placed the T-shirts on a pile next to his desk. "Many people don't believe in evolution, and I was working with Blanchard to give parents an alternative."

"What did you and Blanchard plan?"

"In the next education bill, we were requiring schools to offer alternatives to evolutionary theory and for teachers to say evolution is a theory and not truth. The legislation would require alternative theories, like intelligent design and creationism, be included in standardized tests."

"You've met with resistance." Tim thought to himself that he would be one of the resisters.

"There's this nut group called Keep Evolution in the Schools. They're based in Boston but have cells all around the country, just like the commies did during the Cold War. They've torn down our posters and actually appeared at our committee hearings wearing monkey costumes with heads looking like me. It was disgusting! Look what they did to this poster."

Congressman Bollinger swiveled his chair and swung back, holding a poster showing a hungry-looking cat with its mouth open, teeth bared, and claws sticking out, looking up at an evolutionary dream sequence showing a monkey becoming a man. The caption read: "Evolution: It's Like Catnip for the Scientists."

"Active cells of Keep Evolution in the Schools spray-painted our Satan poster."

"Satan poster?" Tim wanted to end the meeting but didn't want to offend a congressman, since he knew his bosses at the FBI and Homeland Security would be pretty upset.

"It shows a drawing of Satan," Bollinger explained, "with the words, 'Satan Says: You Evolved from a monkey! And if you believe that, I have a global warming crisis to sell you.' Environmental groups are other possibilities for the poisoning and bombing," he continued. "These crazies threatened my committee when we tried to put in Title I a requirement that other ideas on climate change be taught besides those of these radical-commie scientists."

Tim stopped taking notes, trying to determine when it would be polite to leave.

"You've got to get these Greenpeace types. They destroyed all our wonderful Al Gore posters we put outside schools across the country. The poster has a headshot of Gore and the words, 'Not Evil, Just Wrong; The True Cost of Global Warming Is HYSTERIA.' Can you image those commie environmentalists destroying a truthful poster? If they'd go that far, then they should be suspects."

"I can't imagine." Tim shook his head, wanting to change the subject. "What about Brightstone and Kiwi?"

"I hope you're not suggesting they're suspects. They are American companies loyal to our country and agreed before my committee to provide a more balanced curriculum that would value of abstinence education, alternatives to evolutionary theory, and a balanced discussion of climate change. They said these will be in their books, tests, computer tablets, and learning programs. They also mentioned teacher robots could do this."

"Teacher robots! Did they talk about teacher robots with your committee?"

"It was a laugh when my colleague from Iowa suggested they could be models for sex education, since they always practice abstinence." Bollinger laughed. "We did build grants into Title I legislation," the congressman explained, "to fund research and development of these robots; seems ideal to me. You can't trust what teachers are going to say in the classroom. We've heard of wacko teachers supporting premarital sex, evolution, and complaining about the weather. The committee heard from one principal that he walked into a class where the teacher was saying the US government was the government of the rich. With teacher robots we can stamp out this type of hate speech."

"Did any of the Title I money go to Brightstone or Kiwi?" asked Tim.

"Sure, with Secretary of Education Blanchard in charge of spending the money. I know he really liked the two companies and thought they could save American education. I worry that public schools will continue to teach secular ideas and oppose the God-given words of Scripture. The only real thing that will save the schools is a Constitutional amendment allowing for school prayer and Bible reading."

"Do you know anything about the Booker T. Washington Charters or the Common Core Fund?"

"Title I gives money to charters, which are our only hope for saving kids from these godless public schools. But can I be honest with you?"

"Certainly," Tim replied.

"I know these are considered terrorist acts, and Homeland Security has access to NSA data. You know or will find out that my campaign received major donations from Brightstone and Kiwi. You will also discover that the Brightstone and Phillipson foundations have paid for many study trips for members of my family and me. Also, that I'm on the board of directors of the Common Core Fund."

"I don't think that's a problem." Tim immediately began to worry that his investigation would lead to campaign cover-ups and potential bribery issues that could be distractions from the main investigations.

Bollinger sighed. "It's not you and the investigation I worry about but the media getting a hold of this information and using it for political attacks. I assume information in the investigation is kept secret."

"Yes, it is, until we go to court. But I don't think campaign contributions and your overseas trips would ever come up in court."

"There's another thing. I'm also on the board of directors of the Booker T. Washington Charter Schools. That's why they have a pro-America curriculum. Someone might claim a connection between my support of increased charter school funding and being on the board of directors of the Booker T. Washington Schools."

"I doubt if that information would ever come out." Now Tim understood why the congressman was so anxious to talk to the FBI. Bollinger was worried his connections to the education industry could be a political problem.

God, Tim thought, driving away from the federal building, I had no idea so many people were trying to make money off schools. He remembered his good experiences in Detroit public schools, but he had heard Detroit schools were hurt by a lack of money, with the collapse of the car factories.

"You're a welcome sight," he said to Felicia, who was waiting outside the union building for him. "You have no idea all the weird stuff I've been hearing. I can't tell you, because the investigation is secret, but it's like a conspiracy to destroy public schools."

Chapter 9

"I know you can't talk about the investigation." Felicia smiled warmly at Tim Geary over breakfast the next morning in her apartment. "But you did mention on the phone and last night something about people wanting to destroy public schools."

Putting his hand over hers, he said softly, "I'm so glad we met."

"Me too, Tim." Felicia reached over and kissed his cheek. "I'm asking because I'm on a national union committee trying to stop attacks on public schools."

"Good for you." Tim took a sip of his coffee. "I wish I could tell you all the crazy talk against public schools I heard, but I can't."

"I think the teacher robot that guy from Kiwi told me about is part of it. They want to get rid of public-school teachers."

"Have you seen him since the conversation?" Tim felt a twinge of jealousy.

"Haven't seen him since, but my secretary Joyce is dating him. She contacted him out of an interest in getting a certificate in Teacher Robot Operations."

"Teacher robot operations." Tim sighed, thinking he should get the rep's name for the investigation. "What's his name again?"

"Bob Carlson; I think they may be getting serious." Felicia stood up and carried her plate and cup to the sink. "I've got to get ready for work. What about you?"

"I'm going to stop by my house for a change clothes."

"I don't even know where you live. Things happened pretty fast last night."

"Since the Boston Marathon bombing, I've been working out of our Cincinnati office," Tim explained. "I rented a small house near our headquarters on Ronald Reagan Drive."

"We could go there next time. Or will there be a next time?" Felicia headed to her bedroom to dress.

"I hope so." Tim followed her. "Has Joyce said anything about this guy Carlson?"

"Only that he wants to take her to China."

"China—why China?"

"Maybe to impress her." Felicia buttoned her blouse and began rummaging around in her closet for a matching pair of shoes. "She said it was about robotic operations."

"Why would a sales rep be going to China?"

"It turns out—at least, that's what Joyce told me—this Bob Carson is in more than sales. He is some kind of liaison between Brightstone, Kiwi, and the Chinese government. I don't know anything about the China part."

"With that kind of position"—Tim came over and stroked her shoulder—"why was he talking to the school board and then you? By the way, you look really good."

"Thanks; I need to hear that before I go talk to the school superintendent this morning." Felicia began combing her hair. "You might want to ask Joyce. She's talking about moving out of her parents and quitting her job. I think she's getting carried away with Bob. Time will tell."

"Looks like I should see her. Is she always at the union office?"

"She's getting there a little late. Bob's still in town—something about Principal Grinder. The Cincinnati Booker T. Washington

Charter was going to be the first to use the robots. Bob was explaining that to the school board, along with trying to sell them on the idea."

"How do I look?" Felicia turned away from the mirror and faced Bob. "Is my hair okay?"

"It looks great to me!"

Felicia was a little nervous getting out her car in front of the offices for the Cincinnati public schools. Why would the superintendent want to see me? she wondered. We're not due to negotiate until the next fall.

Superintendent Bill Conklin was relatively new to Cincinnati, having left a superintendency position in Bowling Green, Ohio, the year before. He liked his job. He started as a social-studies teacher and became a high-school principal in Cleveland. After getting his doctorate at Cleveland State University, he accepted the position in Bowling Green. A thin, tall, black man in his late forties, he stayed fit with daily exercise. He was active in the local NAACP, and, because of his interest in Cincinnati's National Underground Railroad Freedom Center, he had met the Grinders.

"Always good to see you." Bill got up from his desk to greet Felicia. "We've never had a chance to just chat. I thought, given all the things that are happening, this might be a good time. Did you know that I was very active in the Cleveland teachers union before being a principal?"

"Didn't know that." Felicia smiled at learning he might be pro-union and sat down in the chair he indicated in front of his desk.

"These are difficult times." Bill sat back down. "The bombing was terrible. I know the Grinders, and even though I don't like charter schools, I feel sorry for Carl."

"I guess we agree on charters. Do you know I'm working on the national union's Committee to Save Public Schools? We're worried about the charters." Felicia wondered about Bill as an ally.

"Carl and I have been around and around on charters. He thinks only charters can save poor kids. He thinks public schools are a failure. Now he wants to replace teachers with robots. What a crackpot idea!"

"Well," Felicia responded, wondering where the conversation would go, "I guess we agree on that topic, and I promise not to bring up teachers' salaries."

"I didn't invite you here to negotiate, though I think teacher salaries are way too low, particularly in Cincinnati. I wanted to talk about the Committee to Save Public Schools. President DeWitt Clinton of the School Superintendents Association asked me to talk to you when he heard you were committee chair. The association is interested."

"What?" Felicia almost broke out laughing at the idea of the union working with the superintendents. Most of the time the union and superintendents sat facing each other across a table, arguing about contracts.

"It sounds strange, but these are strange times. In my whole history as student, teacher, principal, and superintendent, I didn't think people would actually try to do away with public schools."

Jesus, Felicia thought, that's what Tim mentioned. "Dr. Conklin, this is the second time I've heard someone say that in the last twenty-four hours."

"All this talk about schools failing poor kids," the superintendent continued. "Just give me the same amount of money some of these charters get from private donors, and we could actually have smaller classes, more in-school and after-school tutoring, and extracurricular activities. We've had to cut arts programs. Now the board wants foreign languages taught by software."

"The union is planning a pro–public schools media blitz," Felicia informed him. "But most media are controlled by anti-union and anti–public school interests. Putting up ads is one thing, but getting on newscasts is another. The news media and politicians like to bash the schools."

Bill sat back in his chair, staring thoughtfully at the ceiling. "I asked to talk to you because a small group of superintendents is interested in working with the union to defeat anti–public school forces. This is not an official group of the School Superintendents Association. We're trying to keep it as much of a secret as possible."

"Why a secret?" Felicia preferred being open about political activities.

"Not all superintendents agree with us," Bill explained. "Some are very right-wing and actually support privatization of schools. The privatization types are mostly former business and military people who were appointed superintendents without any previous educational experience. Some superintendents are afraid to speak out, which is most of our membership, and a handful are just plain dumb. Our small group formed last year, and we've been meeting quietly. Now we're ready to act."

"I'm not authorized to do anything," Felicia responded. "I can't speak for the Committee to Save Public Schools or the union."

"I understand. This meeting is only to ask you to carry a message to your colleagues that we're interested in working together."

"On what, exactly?"

"Our little group—and I'm the only member you will know—has hired a private investigator to look into the financial dealings of Brightstone, Kiwi, and something called the Common Core Fund. Charter school networks like Booker T. Washington are tied to this fund. This web of people and organizations seem to be leading the anti–public school campaign through media contacts and supporting political candidates."

"What about the bombing and poisoning?" Felicia asked. "Secretary Blanchard and the Booker T. Washington Charters seem to be part of the anti–public school group. Who might be targeting them?"

"We think it might be some fringe group," Bill confided. "It certainly, we hope, is not the union, and it is not our group. There are many people upset with what's happening—even pro-choice and environmental groups. Also, we heard there are some technophobes who don't like turning teaching over to software and robots. Then there are the Occupy Wall Street types that think this is a plot to turn schools into private corporations for billionaires to exploit. Then there are anti-testing groups. The possibilities are almost endless, given the enemies created by this takeover of schools."

"Takeover of schools." Felicia was wondering if she should tell Tim about this conversation. "How do you see that happening?"

"Our private investigator found documents, including press statements, which clearly indicate a corporate takeover of schools led by Brightstone and Kiwi, using money from the Common Core Fund. There is big money involved. Over $515 billion is spent on preschool through secondary school education. Over $781 billion is spent, if higher education is included. Corporations are finding higher education a source of revenue through online instruction and privatizing other college functions. Banks love student loans and lobby to increase tuition, so students will borrow more."

"Do you think these are related to the terrorist acts?" asked Felicia.

"It's a mystery who did it, and we have no clues implicating any particular person or organization. But we're not interested in solving those cases. We want to focus on a counter-effort to save public schools."

"How do you see doing this? The union," Felicia explained, "wants to throw support behind pro–public school local, state, and national politicians. The real nut for us to crack is media. They don't want to offend their sponsors or the big money that owns them."

"We're finding the same problem."

"Union people can't get on talk shows," Felicia continued. "News reporters seldom contact union leaders for comments on blatantly anti-school speeches. The union sends op-ed pieces to newspapers that are never printed. We keep running up against a stone wall as far as media is concerned."

"That's why our little group of superintendents wants to work with the union and maybe other education groups. We've got to develop the muscle to stop these people. For instance, we think we can get the NAACP and La Raza involved."

"What do you want me to do or say to the union?" Felicia asked.

"Take them our request to work together. But I must warn you about secrecy."

"Secrecy. I don't think I like to work behind closed doors." Felicia's faced showed her disapproval.

"We found out our meetings were bugged. One member of the group found his home and office had been searched, with his papers scattered around the rooms. The investigator found that our e-mails were being hacked. There are some troubling forces working against us. With a murder and a bombing, some superintendents want to drop out of our circle. They're, frankly, scared."

"Do you actually think this can be done in secret?" Felicia doubted the ability to maintain secrecy, given what she knew about cyberspying.

"The most important thing is not using e-mail or any social media," Bill advised. "We should meet after you've talked to your committee. Given everything else, we probably shouldn't talk in my office or yours. Our investigator actually found a bug in the room where our group met. We should meet in a park or some other public space for a safe conversation."

Chapter 10

"We're going to have to stop all electronic communications," Secretary Alan Olsen of Homeland Security informed Agent Geary over the phone. "Too many probes from China. This will be our last phone contact, unless there is an emergency."

"What'll I do with reports and arranging any meetings?" Tim asked.

"Cybersecurity warns that nothing is safe. They discovered Chinese hackers got into our data files. We will do everything by courier and handwritten notes and reports. At this point we don't need codes, since all communication will pass directly from the sender to a top-secret courier who will hand-deliver messages."

"What about codes on electronic communications?"

"According to cybersecurity," Alan said, "the NSA was able to decipher Chinese-coded e-mails. That means they can do the same to ours."

"Isn't this going to slow everything down? It certainly is going to be difficult for you to approve any trips or interviews I want to make."

"I know. It would be great if we had carrier pigeons rather than couriers flying all over the world." Alan paused, thinking about asking his assistant to check into carrier pigeons.

"Okay." Tim sounded dismayed at these changes. "When can I get messages to you?"

"We're setting up the couriers, and everything should be operational in a couple of days. Don't worry about my approval, until all this is working. Just go ahead and do whatever you were planning."

"You said you wanted everything handwritten?" Tim was happy that his first-grade teacher had focused on cursive writing. "Why not typewriters?"

"We've set up handwriting experts to look at all secret messages to ensure they are from the sender. A typed message can't be checked in this manner."

"This seems like a step backward," Tim commented.

"The reality is that electronic communications and typing are old-fashioned," Alan explained. "Handwriting, letters, and fountain pens are the new future."

"What about air travel? Wouldn't they be able to track me, between credit cards and airport security?" Tim shook his head, thinking how this made his job more difficult.

"You'll have to pay for your tickets in cash. Your ID for ticketing will change for each trip," Alan stated. "We thought of constantly changing credit cards, but that was too complicated. A secret cash fund will be set up at a bank—I can't name it over the phone, because this conversation may be tapped."

"No credit cards, electronic communications, telephones," Tim replied. "Sounds like the modern world is self-destructing. Should I use disappearing ink?"

"We thought of that, but we need to keep all messages for legal reasons. Agent Geary, I'm going to hang up now, and I would like to see you in Washington in two days, where we can talk in our secure room. Just remember to use good penmanship."

"Boss, before you go, when will this happen? I can't do anything without a credit card. I can't even check into hotels."

"Someone will be at your office within the hour. Good-bye." Alan ended the conversation.

Tim sat back thinking about the next interview with Elizabeth Factor, president of the Common Core Fund. He had planned to fly to Chicago that evening and be at her office early in the morning. Also, Alan had ordered him to Washington. But now he couldn't book airline tickets or a hotel room.

He'd printed out Elizabeth Factor's bio from the web. He contemplated the end of web research, since those left computer footprints.

Elizabeth Factor's bio revealed a career focused on exploiting the for-profit side of education. She had a bachelor's degree in education from the University of Indiana and an MBA from Northwestern University. She had been vice-president of marketing for a major publisher before becoming general manager of the for-profit On-Time Learning Corporation. From On-Time Learning she went to Brightstone as president of their elementary textbook division. Then she was hired to head the Common Core Fund, which its website described as, "We look for investments in the education market, particularly in companies involved in online learning, software learning programs, data management, and assessment. We envision an educational future where the use of technology enhances learning and ensures the success of the Common Core State Standards."

Tim had difficulty focusing on Factor's bio, with his mind drifting to memories of the evening with Felicia. He tried to piece together the unfolding network of connections between publishing and technology companies, the US Department of Education, foundations, and investment funds, and their connection to the bombing and poisoning.

A knock on the door and the quick entrance of a pale-looking, thin, white man dressed in a black suit and wearing a black fedora interrupted Tim's thinking. "Alan Olsen sent me." The man in black handed Tim a handwritten note with Olsen's signature. "I'm Mike Spillane, and I will be your personal courier."

Spillane placed an envelope of money on the desk. "You are to use this for airfare, hotels, and food. No credit cards. With the money are a dozen driver's licenses from different states, with your photo. You use one for purchase of plane tickets and airport security and one for a hotel. Destroy each one after you use it. I will provide you with more driver's licenses after you've used these."

Tim stared at Spillane, thinking how incongruous his black suit was with the normal men's wear in Cincinnati. It looked like something out of a twentieth-century Cold War espionage movie.

"And how will I get my written reports to you to take back to Washington?" Tim asked.

"Each time we meet, I will specify the location for the next meeting. I'll meet you in three days near the flying pig statues along the riverfront." Spillane abruptly turned and headed out the door.

Jesus, Tim thought, this is like Memento Park outside of Budapest, with its Soviet-era statues and little theater showing old KGB training films on how to trail someone and snap secret photos.

The next morning Tim was paying cash and showing a Louisiana driver's license for an airline ticket to Chicago. At the reception desk of the Chicago's Conrad Hilton Hotel, Tim produced a California driver's license and informed the clerk he was paying in cash.

"I'm sorry, but we need a credit card for additional expenses," the clerk, obviously surprised that someone would be paying in cash, informed Tim.

"This is legal tender. The law requires you to accept it in payment," Tim snapped back, having rehearsed this scene in his mind.

"Well," the hotel manager said, returning with the front desk clerk after she had scurried off to find out what to do with cash, "you can pay for the room in cash, but we have to disconnect your phone in case of charges, and you will not be able to charge anything to your room."

"That's okay," Tim answered, thinking how the manager and clerk would now clearly remember his face, which might defeat the attempt at secrecy.

Free of all technology—cell phones, computers, tablets, computerized glasses, and wristwatch computers—and armed with a paper notebook and pen, Tim walked to the Common Core Fund offices on Michigan Avenue, near the hotel.

Showing his FBI ID with his real name to the receptionist, Tim stared around at the Fund's slogans: "We Invest in America's Future," "Invest in Ed Tech for Our Children," "Teacher Robots a Good Investment," "Online Learning an Investment in the Future Classroom," "Invest in Charter Schools for Profit and America's Future," and "Analytics Predicts a Student's Future: Invest Now."

"I see you're looking at our investment opportunities." Elizabeth Factor smiled, entering the reception room. "Are you or the FBI thinking of investing in education to secure the country's place in the global economy?"

"No," Tim replied, looking at the still-attractive gray-haired woman in her early sixties, dressed in a smart-looking pin-striped pantsuit. "I want to talk about other matters."

Factor led Tim into her richly furnished office, followed by the receptionist, pushing a cart stocked with glasses, cups, thermoses of coffee and tea, and a full range of liquors.

"Would you like a drink?" Factor offered. "Or can the FBI drink on the job?"

"Coffee is fine," Tim answered, sitting in a high-back leather chair under an original painting by Jasper Johns near the corner table, where the receptionist was arranging his coffee service.

"So what's this all about?" Factor sat down in a red upholstered chair made of carved ebony, on the other side of the serving table.

"I'm here to discuss the poisoning of Secretary Blanchard and the bombing of the Booker T. Washington Charter."

"We're an investment firm trying to save American children. I don't think you'll find much here about those tragedies." Factor poured herself a glass of single-malt scotch.

"According to our records, Secretary Blanchard was on your board of directors."

"Yes, he was here from the beginning and resigned when appointed to the Education Department."

"According to our data"—Tim paused to look at some notes he'd jotted down before leaving Cincinnati—"he still had investments in the Common Core Fund when he died."

"He was always a firm believer in the role of the free market in helping our children. He helped direct some of our fund's original investments," Factor said, sipping on her glass of scotch. "He believed that only technology and for-profit learning companies could save American schools."

"Your fund loaned money to Brightstone and Kiwi, which he was also involved with."

"We've always urged our investors to put money in Brightstone and Kiwi because of their promising future in saving schools. Of course, we also recommend many other online and technology companies."

"What about Booker T. Washington Charter Schools? What is your fund's relationship to Carl Grinder?"

"Marvin Goldman and Abe Stein are on our board of directors, and they are launching Booker T. Washington School Management Company next year. It will contract with public schools to operate them like their charters. Working for profit ensures the company will do the best to help American kids."

"And Grinder?"

"Carl was a consultant with us at the beginning. He helped plan the fund and is still invested in it. He went to work for the Booker T. Washington Charter Schools because of his investments with us and Brightstone and Kiwi. He planned to supervise a Cincinnati school for launching of Kiwi's most important new product: a teacher robot."

"I understand the first test run of the robot in China failed."

"A minor glitch," Factor commented, finishing her drink and pouring another one.

Tim was beginning to wonder about her drinking. Was it a sign of nervousness, or was she an alcoholic?

"We hear it was a major one," Tim said, "something about the robot not being able to handle vomit in a class. The Chinese official Kiwi's been bribing wants a robot that acts with some empathy or sympathy."

"Those fuckin' Chinese," replied Factor, after taking another sip of scotch. "They want a robot that acts like Confucius. You know, 'Do onto others as you would have them do unto you.' Bunch of crap, if you ask me. Teachers shouldn't have empathy. They should just prepare kids for the test. That's why we want a robot. Teachers need to get their emotions out of the classroom and just assess."

Tim was noticing that Factor's speech was slurring. "So when do you think the robot will be ready?" he asked.

"We hope soon."

"Your fund will have financial problems if the robot isn't marketed soon," Tim said, looking at his notes and wondering how he would be able to get this type of information in the future, with Homeland Security most likely disengaging from the web.

"We'll get that robot moving." Factor was now clearly on the verge of drunkenness, as she poured herself a third drink. "Robots are our future, and they'll be the future of the kids. Did I tell you that we only invest to help kids and America?"

"Why do you believe these robots will save the schools?"

"Let me tell you." Factor unsteadily stood up and slightly staggered to her desk and pressed a button, causing a wood panel to slide open and reveal a video screen. "Our robots will not only treat all students equally—they are color-blind—but they will determine their futures."

"Determine their futures?"

"Analytics and big data—that's what we're using to determine investments, and the robots will use it to predict student actions and futures. We'll be able to predict what they'll want to buy and eat when they graduate. The teaching robots are for predicting future consumer markets."

A slide show started on the wall screen, with a photo of a student sitting, working on a computer tablet connected by two-way arrows with boxes market "Big Student Data," "Assessment Goals," and "The Future." In the next slide, a teacher robot was shown next to the student pointing at something on the tablet screen. The caption read, "Working with Robots Is Fun." In the next slide, the student, now dressed in a suit, was getting into a luxury car. The caption read, "Teacher Robots Can Make Your Future Rich." The following slide showed another student dressed in a convict outfit entering a prison. The caption read, "Teacher Robots Will Know if You Are Studying or Not, and Whether Prison is Your Future."

"See," Factor slurred, stumbling as she used a laser pointer to highlight the criminal student. "The tablet and robot are linked to the big national student database. The tablet feeds the student work into the database, and analytic software determines what the student should do next and how well the student will do."

"How can it do that?" Tim watched as Factor downed another drink and removed her suit coat and opened the top button of her blouse.

"Everything about students, their families, their shopping and travel preferences, and all related public records are in the data system. Our analytic programs can predict by the age of ten whether or not a student will be rich or in jail. It can predict what students will buy when they leave school. We already have contracts to sell the results to retail outlets."

"You can predict by the age of ten whether or not a kid will go to prison?" Tim gasped at the implications. "What happens if the analytic software is wrong?"

"It works, but there are other factors to consider." Factor sat down in her desk chair, clearly drunk.

"What other factors?"

"You know, I started drinking this morning when I heard you were coming. I used the analytic software to predict my future. It determined that I would be super rich, with the world's kids using teacher robots. It also predicted another future of me going to jail. When I heard you were coming, I thought I was being arrested."

"Arrested!" Tim exclaimed. He watched her starting to unbutton the rest of her blouse.

"You fuckers should have the information," Factor slurred, kicking off her shoes. "If the teacher robot fails, the Common Core Fund fails, and I go to jail."

"I'm not here to arrest you. I just want to know who you think might have killed the secretary and bombed the school."

Leering at Agent Geary, Factor tried to stand up. "You're handsome in a tough-guy sort of way. What you doin' this evening? I don't know who bombed or killed, but it was no friend of the Common Core Fund or me. This could ruin us. It could undermine the whole project to save American kids and schools. How about us having a little loving?" she slurred.

"We'll be in touch." Tim abruptly ended the interview and stood up, looking down at the pathetic figure of drunken Elizabeth Factor as she slumped across her desk. Heading out the office door, he told the receptionist to go help her boss.

Chapter 11

"How did you get Chang Bao to vomit at the right time?" Li Luan, head of the Technology Planning Team (TPT), asked his assistant Wang Lin, a short, stocky man in his forties. On the same day as Tim's interview with Elizabeth Factor, the TPT was meeting in the department's plainly furnished safe-room on the tenth floor of the Communist Party's headquarters in the Zhongnanhai complex on the western edge of the Forbidden City. Smog obscured the two lakes in the middle of the government complex in what some call the "other forbidden city."

"I gave her a slow-working emetic right after lunch," Wang replied, smiling at the other comrades gathered in the room. "I just didn't know when it would work. We were lucky that she vomited when she did."

"We thought it would ruin the demonstration. Our evaluation of the robot's programming showed it couldn't handle a sick student," said Liao Yiwu, who headed the TPT programming section. The twenty-five-year-old Liao looked flabby from hours sitting in front of computer screens. "The yellow spray of noodles created enough chaos to cause the robot to fail."

"How much longer should we try to delay robot production?" asked Jiang Lijun, a muscular thirty-year-old man in charge of robotics.

"They're getting close to correcting the problem. I talked to Bert and Jennifer Robinson yesterday, and they've programmed the teaching robot to call for assistance if classroom disruption is detected."

"Every delay means more money in our pockets. The Phillipson Foundation will continue to fund us and the army generals until actual production." Luan smiled. "Plus, we want to make this robot act Chinese and not American. They'll be sold all over the world."

"The Hanban office contacted me," Tan Zuoren, public relations officer for the TPT, informed the group. Tan slicked back his hair and covered his well-formed body with stylish suits. He could fit in with any group of PR people anyplace in the world. "They want to use the robots in their Confucius Institutes. They hope to spread Chinese culture and language around the world with teaching robots."

"Sounds like cultural imperialism," Jiang commented. "Didn't we criticize Western countries for exporting their languages and cultures? Now we intend to do it with robots that act Chinese."

"The Hanban sent me their goals," Tan replied, and read from an official : "Benefiting from the UK, France, Germany, and Spain's experience in promoting their national languages, China began its own exploration through establishing nonprofit public institutions that aim to promote Chinese language and culture in foreign countries in 2004: these were given the name The Confucius Institute."

"So they want a Confucian robot to teach in the world's classrooms," Luan commented. "Do they want it to dress and look like Confucius? My cousin Wang Bing is making Ralph Lauren—style clothes for the robot. Should I tell him to switch to traditional Confucian wear?"

"The Hanban doesn't care about the clothes, since the same styles are sold in shopping malls around the world. They think a robot dressed and looking like the original Confucius would freak out kids. They just want the robot to act Chinese and teach the Chinese language."

"A Confucian teaching robot—any thoughts on how we do this?" Luan asked the group.

"I hope we understand," Tan said, "that the Hanban wants us to engage in a cultural war with America, using global teaching robots.

They think we have an advantage, because Kiwi's plant in Jinan is occupied by the People's Liberation Army."

"Did the Ministry of State Security kill the US secretary of education?" Guo Quan, a tall, thin man in his thirties, asked Tan. Guo was the TPT's university liaison and harbored a secret distaste for Communist Party tactics. He often met secretly with dissident university professors at a teahouse near the Drum Tower.

"Why would you ask a question like that?" Luan wondered.

"As I understand it," Guo explained, "the US Secretary of Education Paul Blanchard wanted teaching robots to spread pro-American ideas about free markets and democracy. This would make the robots a key part of American cultural diplomacy. Killing Blanchard would remove one general in the culture wars."

"We shouldn't speculate on this," Tan warned. "Our task is to ensure that the robots carry out the wishes of our leaders."

"What will this mean in practice?" asked Liao. "I need to know what the Hanban has in mind, so that I can develop a program for the teaching robot."

"The Hanban wants the robot to promote 'Socialism with Chinese characteristics' along with Chinese culture and language," Tan said.

"We know free-market theories will lead to unequal educational opportunities," Luan said firmly. "Only communism will deliver equal chances for an education. The glorious People's Revolution must triumph."

"What about the bombing of that school that was to be the first to use teaching robots?" asked Guo, who wanted to continue discussing the political aspects of the teaching robot. "Was the Ministry of State Security involved?"

"Any discussion of the bombing or poisoning is speculative," Luan snapped. "Let's focus on making a Confucian teaching robot."

"How are we going to do that?" Liao asked. "Kiwi owns the robot, and I don't think Bert Robinson will want a robot to teach socialism with Chinese characteristics."

"I heard Blanchard describe plans to teach free-market ideas to save the world last time I visited the United States," Jiang interjected.

"All those people at Kiwi are pro-American free-marketers. I don't see them allowing robots to be programmed to teach socialism with Chinese characteristics."

"Ah," said Luan in a conspiratorial tone, "but we control Kiwi's factory. Or should I say, the People's Liberation Army controls it."

"Yes," exclaimed Tan, "our glorious leaders knew that if we convinced Americans and Europeans to move their factories here for our cheap labor, we would end up controlling the world's manufacturing! In reality, Kiwi must submit to us, since we occupy their Jinan factory."

"We've got to be a little crafty in our approach," Luan warned. "Kiwi could move the robotic operation back to the United States, plus, the US government will not be happy if they find out we're intending to use the teaching robots to spread our ideas."

"But Secretary Blanchard and the US government were planning to use the robots as part of their plan for cultural imperialism," Tan said. "Why can't we?"

"We will have to work secretly for the robot's programming to be Chinese," Jiang said. "I'm going down to Jinan tomorrow to talk to Bert. He believes we can work together to make the final improvements on the robot. I think Liao Yiwu should go with me and consult with Jennifer about programming robotic emotions."

"I'll go," Liao agreed. "But those Americans seem to want all emotions out of the classroom. That certainly doesn't meet the empathy requirements of a Confucian teaching robot."

"I want you two," Luan commanded, "to change the robot's program, so that it can teach in both English and Mandarin. The Hanban office recognizes that we are in a race to replace English with Chinese as the world language. Whatever language the robot speaks will become the language of global classrooms."

"Is the Ministry of State Security aware of this plan?" asked Guo, looking uncomfortable at the proposal. "What happens if the world chooses English and never uses the Chinese program?"

"The Ministry of State Security is working with the Hanban," Luan informed the group.

"Then they did kill Secretary Blanchard!" exclaimed Guo.

"You must stop suggesting that," ordered Luan. "Let's just plan our strategy."

"I could slip a virus in the robot's program, so that the English program shuts down after six months," Liao offered. "By that time schools will have invested in the robots and will only have ones that speak and teach Chinese."

"Can you imagine the Americans," Tan laughed, "stuck with Chinese-speaking robots? Maybe we can make Chinese the official language of America."

"What about teaching the world socialism with Chinese characteristics?" Luan asked.

"We're supplying the Chinese language program to Kiwi," Liao explained. "In the program, math word problems, and history and literary studies, favor socialism over free-market thinking."

"Those US fascists will go crazy if they learn the teacher robot is programmed to teach socialism with Chinese characteristics," said Tan, standing up and stretching. He found it hard to go so long without tea or other refreshments, which were forbidden, to maintain the security of the safe room.

"I'm also pressuring Jennifer Robinson to program empathy into the robot. I don't think this will be possible, and I agree with her that this emotion might be dangerous," Liao explained, "but it will give us another way to control the robot's programming by slipping in what I call a Confucian chip."

"Why dangerous?" asked Luan. "I thought we requested it after the vomit caper."

"Jennifer convinced me that robots with empathy might unite." Liao yawned, tired of sitting in the stuffy safe room. "With their communications abilities, emphatic teaching robots could form unions or even armies."

"What happens if Kiwi or the American government finds out about what we are doing?" Guo asked.

"First, our army controls the factory," Luan explained. "If anything goes wrong, the Ministry of State Security will arrest Bert and Jennifer Robinson as enemies of the state. Secondly, we can just take over the Kiwi factory and make our own robots. But it would be easier if Kiwi did it, because their global reputation will open doors for selling the teacher robot. Then we control the money."

"How's that possible?" asked Wang.

"The Ministry of Finance has been quietly investing in something call the Common Core Fund. This is an investment firm loaning money to Kiwi and the publishing giant Brightstone to develop the teacher robot," Luan explained. "In essence, the Chinese government can indirectly control both companies. We hear that the Common Core Fund is in trouble after Chang Bao threw up. They are having a cash-flow problem. The Ministry of Finance believes we can exploit the situation to ensure that a Confucian teacher robot appears on world markets. Or should I say, a Confucian teacher robot teaching an English language program that fails if Jiang Lijun is able to put a virus in the robot's program."

"Wang read a summary of the proposals so far," Luan ordered his assistant. "I don't think I can sit in this room much longer."

"This is my list." Wang began to read. "We will delay production of the teacher robot, so that we can assure personal financial benefits for ourselves and the generals. Liao Yiwu will introduce a virus in the robot's program that will after six months destroy the English program. Working with the Hanban office, we will place programs in the robot that will result in the global spread of Chinese language and culture. It will convince the world's students that socialism with Chinese characteristics is superior to free-market economics. We will work with the Ministry of Finance to ensure control of Kiwi, Brightstone, and the Common Core Fund."

"Good," said Luan. "There is one more thing from the Ministry of State Security. It appears that the US government's Homeland

Security is no longer using electronic communications in any form. All communications will be handwritten and sent by special couriers. This seriously limits the ability of the Ministry of State Security to monitor Americans. As a result, and because of the importance of the teacher robot in our war against American cultural imperialism, we will be doing the same thing. No more use of the Internet, e-mail, or phones. Everything will be handwritten. Practice your calligraphy."

"What?" gasped Tan. "I've only used keyboards my whole life. I can't do calligraphy."

"Well, this is the future," Luan responded. "Get yourself a calligraphy pen or brush. The Ministry of State Security is supplying experts to ensure that all handwritten messages are from the correct person. Also, remove all electronics from your homes. In fact, I think we should program the robot to teach Chinese calligraphy. The future of our culture and nation is in our hands."

Chapter 12

Agent Geary passed his handwritten notes across the table to Secretary Olsen, as they sat in Homeland Security's safe room, discussing the investigation. Tim had flown directly from Chicago after interviewing Elizabeth Factor.

Alan complimented the agent. "Tim, you're our best, and I might say, after the Boston bombing, our most gifted investigator. I just want this group to hear this before we proceed. I am confident that you will help all of us to put together the pieces of the investigation."

"Thank you, boss," said Tim, smiling, "but I'm only starting to map out possible suspects. I'm waiting to hear from others, particularly about possible China connections. I haven't had time to chase down foreign suspects."

"We've traced the attempted hacking of our data base to the Technology Planning Team of the Chinese Communist Party," replied Eliot Spooner, a twenty-eight-year-old blond man in charge of Homeland Security's Cyber-Spying Department. Eliot was recruited from the MIT faculty when Homeland Security recruiters learned of his brilliant hacking skills.

"This is the same group involved in Kiwi's teacher-robot project, which has been linked to the bombing. At this point we can't find any connections to the poisoning," said Floyd Henderson, Homeland Security's top data analyst. While at Duke University, Floyd, an overweight African-American with diabetes, had shown a gift for using analytics to squeeze meaning out of large data sets.

"What about possible suspects?" Alan asked Agent Geary.

"I think the first question is why the bombing and poisoning." Tim addressed the small group. "If we could answer the 'why' question, then it would be easier to narrow the investigation."

"What came out of your meeting with Congressman Bollinger?" Alan asked. "He's been calling daily, complaining about our slow progress in finding the culprits."

"A lot of what Bollinger said reflects his political views, which he seems to have shared with Secretary Blanchard," Tim explained. "Basically, he believes there were well-organized groups targeting Blanchard because of Blanchard's agenda of privatization of public schools, free markets, and technology, along with abstinence education. He also identified groups supporting evolution and environmental organizations pressuring the schools to deal with climate change. He also suggested anti-testing and anti–Common Core groups as possibilities."

"Bollinger's politics are an issue." Alan grimaced. "The groups he identified all seem to be on education's liberal side. He never mentions any conservative organizations like the Tea Party or the Aryan Nation."

"I've only looked at the data for groups on Bollinger's list." Floyd looked up from his written notes. "Our team is investigating websites, reading e-mails, and listening to phone messages. All of this takes time. I have ten people mining Bollinger's list. I'll have the team look at conservative groups."

"I think this should be next on your agenda," Alan instructed. "Some conservatives are high on our terrorist list. Remember that Militia sympathizers and right-wing flag-wavers Timothy McVeigh and Terry Nichols bombed the Oklahoma City federal building."

"I'll follow up on this," Eliot affirmed. "We have spies in the most violent prone right-wing groups. I'll find out if any have been active or concerned with education issues. I can get back to the group in a couple of days."

"Floyd," Alan directed. "Please tell us what you found out about the groups on Bollinger's list."

"Sifting through the data, I've identified several of groups on Bollinger's list," Floyd explained, "who sent hostile messages to Blanchard and other members of the Department on Education. They also maintain web pages calling for action against testing and the Common Core. One very active group is Rescue Our Schools, which has staged yearly marches here in Washington."

Tim made a note of the group on his pad of yellow legal paper. "Did you find anything that suggests the members knew how to use ricin, explored its use on the web, or discussed ways to get the poison to Blanchard?" Tim asked.

"Our team sifted through telephone and e-mail messages of all members, along with looking at the subjects of their web searches. We came up with nothing," answered Floyd. "We did find some members who were in prison for felonies and some who were avoiding arrest. One teacher in the group was convicted of fondling a student but escaped to another state. We notified the local police, and he is now in jail."

"What about other groups?" Tim asked. "Also, I would like authorization to send other agents to talk to members of Rescue Our Schools and any other organizations we might identify."

"You can have all the agents you want," Alan replied. "This investigation is of interest to the CIA and the State Department over concerns about a global culture war. The State Department informed me that Secretary Blanchard, just prior to his death, created a Global Education Bureau within the Education Department to conduct a secret cultural offensive through world schools. This bureau was working secretly with Kiwi on programming teacher robots."

"As I will explain," Tim responded, "the Global Education Bureau seems to fit into the networks I've been looking at. But before discussing this, I would like to hear more from Floyd about what his data told him about other groups."

"There is an ecoterrorist group called Hug Our Trees, based in Oregon," Floyd continued. "They've sent threatening e-mails to the Education Department about the lack of emphasis on environmental education."

"Threatening in what sense?" Tim asked.

"Mainly they've threatened to picket the department and, before his death, Blanchard's speeches. They claim Blanchard was working with oil companies to limit discussions of climate change and pollution in schools. In fact, Blanchard did not submit a budget to Congress for continued funding of environmental education, and he never appointed anyone to carry out the existing mandates."

"Has Hug Our Trees ever committed any violent acts?" Tim asked.

"A decade ago members burned down a California Humvee dealership and destroyed heavy-duty machinery at a shopping-mall construction site in New Jersey. Most recently, they organized protests against an oil pipeline in North Dakota and fracking in Pennsylvania, resulting in arrests. But they aren't as violent the No More Growth organization."

"What does this group have to do with the Department of Education?" Eliot asked. "I've been watching them since they burned down the headquarters of Virginia's pro-life organization for supporting a law requiring vaginal ultrasounds before an abortion. They also dumped packets of condoms from planes over Miami. One condom packet blinded a woman when she was hit in the eye jogging in South Beach."

"They were pressuring Secretary Blanchard to distribute lesson plans on population growth and birth control and to end abstinence education programs," Floyd explained. "They appeared before Congressman Bollinger's committee, demanding the distribution of condoms and birth-control pills in schools. They wanted funding for family-planning centers in high schools."

"Did either of you," asked Tim of Floyd and Eliot, "find anything that would suggest they wanted to kill Blanchard or were capable of bombing?"

"Besides the burning of the pro-choice building," Eliot answered, "they did cause a riot, resulting in injuries, protesting a Louisiana bill requiring police approval for unmarried couples to buy birth-control products. Two pro-life advocates were hospitalized in critical condition."

"Good Lord," Tim reacted, "was the bill ever passed?"

"No," Eliot answered. "Later, leaders of the group were arrested in Atlanta, Georgia, for throwing pig fetuses at pro-life picketers who were seeking to limit abortions and the sale of birth-control devices. It's still a mystery where they got the fetuses. One pig fetus hit the windshield of a passing car, causing the driver to lose control and plow into a police car. The driver is still hospitalized, supposedly for the trauma of seeing a flying animal fetus."

"Next you'll tell me they're somehow linked to China." Tim smirked.

"China is in the picture. Every year they try to get Congress to pass a one-child law similar to China. They've petitioned the Department of Education to support educational programs to teach the value of couples' having only one child. Leaders of No More Growth make frequent trips to China to study their one-child policies. They've brought Chinese experts to the United States to advise their group on limiting the population."

"Any particular group in China they've been working with?" asked Tim.

"They've had many contacts with China's National Population and Family Planning Commission. From the data I uncovered, this commission contacted a government office, called the Hanban, to work with the leaders of No More Growth. The head of the National Population and Family Planning Commission decided that China's one-child policy should be part of the Hanban's efforts to spread Chinese culture and language. The commission thinks the one-child policy should be a model that will demonstrate to the world the value and meaning of socialism with Chinese characteristics."

Tim wrote down the linkage between No More Growth and China. "Hasn't the Hanban created Confucius Institutes, such as the one at Bloomberg University in New York and in other countries?"

"Yes, and in the data we were able to collect, the Hanban is engaged in a war of cultural imperialism. They see a global culture war with the United States. The one-child policy is in stark contrast to the policies of US pro-life groups."

"Anything else I should know about this group?" Tim continued writing down Eliot's information.

"Only that they helped distribute Confucian Condoms in Africa."

"Confucian Condoms," Tim asked, "is that a brand-name or a special type?"

"It's a brand-name used by the Chinese government. Each condom has a picture of Confucius printed on its tip, and each wrapper has a Confucian saying."

"I'll assign an agent to visit the leaders of No More Growth." Tim looked up from his writing and asked, "Any other groups that might want to harm the Secretary?"

"There's an anti-testing group based in Philadelphia called Stop Testing," Eliot answered. "They are best known for distributing outside schools T-shirts to students and teachers when state standardized tests are being given. Some T-shirts carry a message that all teachers and students should cheat. There are a couple for teachers, with one saying, 'Save America, Give Your Students the Answers,' and another saying 'Save Our Jobs, Change Student Answers.' A special one for students urges, 'Boycott the Test.'"

"Doesn't sound violent," Tim commented.

"Last year a Texas branch of the organization broke into a Brightstone Test Center and poured acid on all the Texas third-grade answer sheets before they could be scored," Eliot continued. "The most daring was an Illinois branch that hijacked an armored truck carrying all the Chicago state tests to a scoring center in St. Louis. Luckily, no one was harmed. The guard's gun jammed when the group forced their way aboard when the truck stopped at a red light on State Street. The driver and guard were let go in a cornfield near Kankakee, Illinois, and the answers sheets were dumped in the Illinois River."

"I guess they are violent." Tim wrote down some notes. "How did this group feel about Secretary Blanchard?"

"There were unending hate messages," Floyd said, "when I sifted through the data, which included phone and e-mail messages. Members wrote angry messages to each other, denouncing Blanchard's support of testing policies. A great deal of hostility was expressed toward Brightstone, which makes and scores most of the state tests."

"That fits with events in Georgia," Eliot added. "They threw tomatoes and booed the secretary. One demonstrator held an obscene sign that showed the secretary and a woman with Brightstone written on her body, making love. The caption read, 'They're in Bed Together.' The police arrested the demonstrator and destroyed the sign for violating Georgia's public obscenity laws. This led to a scuffle between police and members of Georgia's Stop Testing branch. Two policemen and fourteen demonstrators were hospitalized after tear gas and rubber bullets were used when the demonstrators were joined by teachers and students from a local school. This is a group prone to violent acts."

"Tim, can you add anything from your investigation?" Alan interrupted.

"I just left the office of Elizabeth Factor of the Common Core Fund. She was very distraught and worried about going to jail. I've also looked at the connections among the Common Core Fund, Brightstone, and Kiwi. All three backed the secretary and the Booker T. Washington Charter Schools. There are close ties between all three organizations and the Department of Education. I cannot at this time see any reason why their staff would want to harm the secretary or the charter school. However, there is the issue of the teacher robot."

"I've analyzed a lot of data on Kiwi's teacher-robot project," said Floyd. "It appears that the project failed last week, resulting in the possibility of a financial meltdown of the Common Core Fund. Plus, the Chinese are involved."

"China is closed off now," Eliot interjected. "They are following our lead and abandoning all electronic communications. They're also using handwritten notes. We may have to recruit real spies to replace our cybersecurity efforts. One thing we did find out is that government officials are receiving bribes from the Phillipson Foundation to protect Kiwi's Jinan plant against a workers' revolt."

"I should explain the importance of the teacher-robot project to American security," Alan said. "The State Department informed me that Secretary Blanchard was having the robot programmed to carry the messages of democracy, free markets, and English to the world's classrooms. The State Department considers the teacher robot to be our major weapon in the culture wars. Now they're worried about Chinese involvement in the project."

"Global culture wars." Tim sighed. "How much more complicated can this investigation get?"

"Well, the last message we intercepted suggests the Chinese understand the importance of the teacher robot in the culture wars," Eliot added. "They want the robot to carry their message to the world. I think the teacher robot should be considered vital to our nation's security. Also, I might add, one message suggests they want a Confucian teacher robot."

"Don't they already have Confucian tipped condoms to win the culture wars?" Floyd giggled. "Maybe the State Department should distribute condoms with Uncle Sam on the tip."

"Who's going to handle the Chinese involvement?" Tim asked. "It falls outside my jurisdiction."

"We weren't prepared for the shutdown of electronic communications," Alan said. "We're training spies now. It's a problem to recruit American Chinese who can do calligraphy. But we hope that within a week we can have someone infiltrating the Communist Party's Technology Planning Team."

"I will assign agents"—Tim paused to look at his written list of projects—"to follow up on the organizations we discussed. I will be returning to Cincinnati tomorrow and talking to the local union official, Felicia Cochran, about a national union group she's heading to save public schools." Tim paused as images of his night with Felicia flooded through his brain. "Supposedly this group plans to link itself to a secret group of school superintendents. While I hate to consider the idea, the superintendents association and the union are still suspects in the bombing and poisoning. When should I return to Washington?"

"We should plan to meet here in three days, when, I hope, Eliot will give us a rundown of any right-wing groups interested in school policies," Alan instructed them. "By then I'll have more information from the CIA and the State Department about this global culture war. You may laugh, but I will suggest the Uncle Sam–tipped condom, particularly for Africa. Those Chinese are pretty smart with their Confucian condom. Maybe whoever controls the teaching robot controls the world's culture."

Chapter 13

"Our union group received this in the mail." Felicia handed Tim a letter emblazoned with a Nazi swastika. She took a sip of her tortilla soup at Cincinnati's Nada restaurant, waiting for Tim's reaction.

"When did you get this?" Tim gasped, reading the violent anti-union message. "Was it sent just to your group to save public schools, union leaders, or to all union members?"

"Just to me and the union leadership; I don't know how they found out about us. Should I be worried?"

Tim scanned the note that was put together with words pasted from newspapers and magazines. Some of the more extreme words were from a computer printer. The letter indicated it was sent from the National Headquarters of the Silvershirts and Whiteperson Association. A large swastika was centered at the top of the page, and the text was surrounded by circular symbols displaying American flags with Christian crosses on them.

"I'll check this out, but don't worry about it for now," Tim tried to convince her. "There're all sorts of creeps around the country."

"But it threatens me and the union."

"Threats like this appear all the time, I can assure you."

"Why does it target me and the union as racists? Why do they suggest bodily harm for helping minority students? Why do they call us anti-Christian and anti-American? I've heard the Common Core called many things but not racist, anti-Christian, and un-American. Where does this thinking come from?"

"Can I keep this letter and the envelope? I'll look into the organization and trace the letter," Tim said, as Felicia's soup dish was replaced with pork-and-green-chili-pepper enchiladas, and he was served a grilled adobo-rubbed pork chop.

"I've missed you," Tim added. "All this investigative travel makes it difficult."

"How'd you get into FBI work?" Felicia said, after relishing the taste of the enchilada.

"I went to Michigan State on a football scholarship, without any particular job goals." Tim took a bite of his pork chop. "This is pretty good. How's yours?"

"Delicious, but continue the story."

"I think I told you my father worked in a Detroit car factory and held some low-level positions in the United Auto Workers. That's why I tend to be pro-union. We never had much money, and the family assumed I would follow in my father's footsteps. But I did well as a fullback in high school, and I was recruited to Michigan State on a football scholarship."

"You've got the build to be a football player." Felicia looked admiringly at Tim.

"I never liked jocks and hung out with more studious types. The pro teams tried to sign me up after college, but I couldn't face a life of locker rooms and sports talk." Tim downed his glass of tequila and waved at the waitress for a refill.

"You could have been a professional player earning big money, and you ended up in the FBI. That's quite a choice."

"I was accepted by the University of Michigan law school. My scores on the law-school entrance exam were high, so they gave me a free ride. Somehow I graduated with honors."

"Why aren't you at some big-time law firm?"

"I never fit in with the law-school crowd. They were the extreme opposite of the jocks. All they talked about was landing the big job and making money. They never seemed to care about anything but grades and money."

Felicia asked a passing waitress for more Mexican beer to wash down the enchiladas. "What's wrong with more money?"

"That's not how I grew up." Tim took the last bite of his pork chop and put down his knife and fork. "My family was very political, always rooting for the underdog. They hated lawyers and said that justice worked only for the rich. All my upbringing worked against my joining a hotshot law firm. I guess I could have become a public defender."

"Why didn't you?" Felicia asked, as the waitress cleared away their plates and handed them dessert menus.

"My background is somewhat like yours." Felicia continued. "Both my parents worked on the jet-engine assembly line at the local General Electric plant. They were also pro-union and hoped I would go to law school. They would have wanted me to be a public defender. But I decided teaching would help me serve others."

"FBI recruiters showed up on campus," Tim explained, "and I took the easy way to a job and signed up."

"What did your parents think? I know mine would have been upset if I even considered the FBI." Felicia studied the dessert menu. "I think I'll have the chocolate torte—it sounds yummy—with the bananas foster gelato and Myers's dark rum caramel."

"They were furious, particularly my father, who hated the FBI because of Hoover's persecution of unions. But I thought of it as hunting down the bad guys to help society." Tim glanced up from the menu. "I'm going to have the butterscotch flan."

"And, you became a hero in Boston."

"Sort of—now the FBI and Home Security contacts me on any possible terrorist case. Also, my parents were proud about Boston and finally accepted my being an FBI agent."

"How come you're single?" Felicia had been waiting all evening to ask this question.

"Never got serious in school, there was too much work between football and studying and then law school. Don't get me wrong; I had girlfriends, but I could never imagine them as lifetime mates."

"And as an FBI agent, you must have attracted a horde of women."

"I don't think a *horde*. FBI life doesn't allow much time for relationships. I travel a lot, and I just never met the right person. What about you?"

"Married after getting my teacher certificate to the principal of the school where I did my student teaching. It lasted a year. He turned out to be abusive and was eventually arrested when he was discovered watching on a web cam the girls' soccer team shower. I've been single ever since."

Finished with their desserts, they eyed each other. Finally, Tim asked, "Would you like to see my house?"

* * *

Tim put Felicia's letter in an evidence envelope to take to Washington. He wished he'd had the letter when he met the secret courier yesterday afternoon by the flying pigs along the river. They'd arranged another meeting after Tim returned from Washington in two days.

Two of the Booker T. Washington teachers contacted his office, asking to be interviewed. Tim had read over all teachers' statements to the Cincinnati police and didn't find anything of interest. He wondered what these two teachers knew that led them to directly contact the FBI.

Blanch Cooper and Eric Somers nervously entered his office and took the seats Tim indicated at the little conference table in the corner of the room.

"Were either of you hurt? This was a terrible tragedy." Tim looked sympathetically at them.

"We asked to see you because of Principal Grinder," Eric blurted out. "I must tell you that I was barely getting by until the bombing.

With the school closed, I'm earning nothing and may lose my house. My wife has left, taking the kids to Florida."

"Don't you have a contract? Aren't they still paying you?" Tim asked.

"We haven't a union, and the Booker T. Washington Charter Schools refuses to pay us," Blanch said, on the verge of tears. "I'm a single mom with kids, and I don't know what we'll do for money."

"They're not honoring your salaries after all you've been through." Tim looked surprised. "But let's hear what you have to say about Principal Grinder. What's this have to do with the bombing?"

"The day before the bombing," Eric explained, "Grinder had us locked away, changing answers on student tests. He was worried that the charter school would get a poor rating by the state."

"I've heard of the practice," Tim said. "It's one advocated by the group Stop Testing. Do you two belong?"

"Definitely not!" Blanch exclaimed. "They're a bunch of left-wingers. I believe in tests but not in changing student answer sheets. Grinder couldn't face the fact that the kids from that neighborhood would never to do well in school or on tests. The whole goal of the Booker T. Washington Charters is hogwash. They'll never save these kids with all those phony sayings from Washington's book *Up From Slavery* they plastered all over the school walls."

"It's what we saw in the storage room that we want to talk about," Eric said. "There was a box there addressed to Grinder and covered with all sorts of Chinese symbols and Chinese stamps—"

"When I saw it," Blanch interrupted, "I knew that left-winger was working for the Chinese Communists."

"How did you know it was from the Communist Party?" Tim asked.

"We didn't know," Eric answered. "But there were stickers with the Chinese flag."

"His secretary told me"—Blanch leaned forward, looking directly into Tim's eyes—"that the principal had a lot of contact with China and flew there frequently."

"My pastor constantly warns us about Chinese brainwashing and their desire to take over the world," Eric added. "I believe there is a plot to change this country from a God-fearing capitalist country into a communist-atheist state. And we think that box contained the bomb. Grinder did it."

"Why would he want to blow up his own school?" Tim asked.

"He knew it was failing, and all the government promises about equality of educational opportunity were foolhardy falsehoods," Eric answered. "Look at his wife; she works for that commie National Underground Railroad Freedom Center. Those coloreds are always causing problems."

"How is that?" Tim made some notes on the conversation for the Washington meeting in two days on conservative groups.

"If they had just waited and not started the Civil War and ended slavery, they would now be free and rich. They were still ignorant African savages back then. They needed slavery to civilize them," Eric explained. He and Blanch agreed on this subject.

"Let me understand you." Tim was quickly writing down the conversation. "You think the bomb was in the box from China and that somehow Grinder was responsible."

"That's right," Blanch agreed. "None of this would have happened if they still had school prayer."

"What does school prayer have to do with the bombing?" Tim looked quizzically at the two.

"We all know," Blanch claimed, "that the schools went downhill after the sixties. Between the hippies and the Supreme Court, our God-fearing schools were doomed. Of course, integration didn't help. Colored kids need their own schools. They like to be with their own kind. They need to learn how to act before being put in schools with whites."

"I still don't understand how this explains the principal wanting to blow up his own school."

"By throwing out school prayer and the Bible, the Supreme Court turned public schools into godless institutions," Eric said. "How can you teach morals and good character without God in the classroom?"

"These charter schools aren't going to help these colored kids without God being there," Eric added. "These Negroes need discipline if they're ever to free themselves from what happened because of the Civil War. The only true discipline comes with God's words."

"The point is," Blanch said, "our school was failing, and Grinder knew it. He had to blow it up to save his career."

"What if I told you"—Tim looked at the two—"that Grinder is independently wealthy and financially doesn't need the school."

"I don't think that matters, because he is working for the godless Chinese." Blanchard sounded irritated at Grinder questioning their statements. "His real career is destroying our way of life by preaching equality, just like the Communists."

"What about the poisoning of Secretary Blanchard? Do you see any connection?" This flood of racist statements was making Tim uncomfortable, and he wanted to change the subject.

"We haven't discussed that," Eric said, looking at Blanch. "I don't know if Grinder is connected, but the secretary was another reason to worry about schools teaching Big Brother ideas."

"How's that?" Tim asked.

"He wanted the federal government to control the minds of our children," Eric explained. "That's what the Common Core is all about. Commies trying to brainwash our kids."

"I'm sure he liked the secretary," Blanch added. "Grinder was always talking about the federal government's helping poor kids."

"The only way we'll save the schools is to get the feds out of education, and bring back school prayer and the Bible." Eric was almost yelling. "Stop talking about equality and all those other godless, communist ideas. The schools should educate God-fearing patriots."

"I want to thank you for this information." Tim stood up, indicating the meeting was over. "I will report all this to Homeland Security."

"Don't forget that Chinese box it contained the bomb," Eric reiterated. "Those millions of Chinese will be marching through our lands, killing, and raping our women. We're sure Grinder is an agent of the Chinese Communist Party."

Chapter 14

After giving instructions to other FBI agents in Cincinnati to visit the leadership of the organizations identified at the Homeland Security meeting, Tim headed to the airport to visit Horton University. One Horton faculty name kept appearing on documents from Kiwi and Brightstone. He used cash to hire a driver at the San Francisco airport, since he couldn't rent a car without a credit card.

A secretary ushered Tim into the office of Professor Philip Riesling, who held the Brightstone Chair in Learning and Technology. The endowed Brightstone Chair provided Riesling with a large travel budget plus a supporting staff of six faculty researchers and their assistants. Riesling was famous in the education world for his 1990 University of Wisconsin dissertation published a year after his graduation, as *The Technology of Learning*. The book won the Kiwi Award for contributions to education and one from the American Educational Research Association. Basically, the book said that technology could do a better job teaching than could humans.

Recognizing the value of Riesling's work to their bottom line, Kiwi funded Riesling to produce more studies supporting the conclusion of his dissertation. Kiwi's funding helped Riesling secure a position in 1992 at Horton University. At Horton, Riesling and a team of graduate research students began producing an average of ten coauthored papers a year that were published in education journals and presented at major conferences. While most of the research and writing was done by the graduate students, they accepted Riesling listing himself as major author with them as the second authors. The students hoped that just having their names associated with Riesling would launch their careers.

The quality and quantity of Riesling's scholarly production increased in 1998, when Brightstone provided his endowed chair with funds to hire young faculty members instead of graduate students. Like the graduate students, faculty members starting their career were happy to be listed as secondary authors, just to have their names associated with Riesling's. In 2001, with Riesling being listed as chief editor, his researchers published the now famous and groundbreaking collection of essays, *Making the Classroom Work: How Technology and Assessment Will Save American Schools.*

After the book's publication, Kiwi and Brightstone hired a public relations firm to spread the word that testing and technology would save schools. Conferences speeches, television interviews, and consulting work with state education departments and the US Department of Education filled Riesling's schedule. Opinion pieces, written by the public relations firm listing Riesling as the author, appeared in newspapers, magazines, and education journals around the world. Honorary degrees from world universities began to cover Riesling's office walls.

Riesling stood at Paul Blanchard's side when he was sworn in as secretary of education. While they shared a personal dislike for each other, Riesling and Blanchard learned to work together through their mutual contacts and funding from Brightstone and Kiwi.

Riesling was feared in the academic world because of the many careers he had destroyed when his work was challenged. Anthony Carlyle discovered this when, as an assistant education professor at the University of Illinois, he gave a paper at the American Educational Research Association demonstrating the faulty statistical methods used in Riesling's original work, *The Technology of Learning*. Carlyle also had the audacity to point out that Riesling had not published anything since his original book that was not coauthored by a research assistant.

Using his political and academic influence, particularly with the education dean at Illinois, who was dependent on Riesling's network to earn twice his income in consulting work, Riesling ensured that Carlyle was denied tenure and forced to leave the university and that he was not hired at any university or four-year college. Carlyle spent the rest of his career with a heavy teaching load at a Springfield, Illinois, community college. The story of Carlyle's encounter with Riesling ended all criticism of Riesling's work.

Tim looked admiringly at the awards and honorary degrees adorning Riesling's office looking out on Horton's main quad. Tim immediately disliked Riesling, who, unlike other of Horton's education faculty, wore expensive and well-tailored pinstripe suits. A short white man with a pot belly, Riesling's personal hair stylist kept him groomed in the latest styles from *Gentleman's Quarterly*. One reason for Tim's negative impression was Riesling's pretentious British accent. From reading his file, Tim knew the accent must be phony, since Riesling was born in Omaha, Nebraska, and had spent only a couple of months in London lecturing. Many of Riesling's colleagues were afraid to comment on his new accent when he returned from his brief visit to the UK.

"You know why I'm here," Tim said, sitting down across the desk from Riesling. "You were good friends with Secretary Blanchard, and I want your thoughts on who might have wanted to poison him."

"Good friends is an exaggeration." Riesling smirked. "We worked together on a number of projects, and I did consulting work with the Department of Education after he was appointed. We never met socially."

"From our reports, and I should mention that investigators have access to the National Security Agency's database; both you and Blanchard frequently met at the Kiwi and Brightstone headquarters."

"Of course, we were both dedicated to ensuring the success of the Common Core and classroom technology. Our work at Brightstone demonstrates their importance and Kiwi's for improving American schools. Both companies prized our guidance."

"Can you tell me anything about why Blanchard was appointed secretary of education after playing professional hockey in Canada and a brief period as a remedial reading teacher in a Chicago charter school? In fact, I can find nothing that shows Blanchard had any remedial reading training."

"Well," Riesling said, looking slightly contemptuous, "I don't like speaking unkindly of the dead, but you're right he had no qualifications to be secretary. It was because he played hockey in college with Bridgestone's President John Greenwood. After damaging his leg and retiring from sports, Blanchard contacted his old friend Greenwood, who set him up in Chicago using Brightstone's new Save the Poor reading program."

"Why would Greenwood do that, given Blanchard's background?"

"There were rumors that their college relationship was more than a mere friendship. Bridgestone's marketing department wanted to promote Blanchard at teachers' meetings as a major sports star who used the Save the Poor reading program. That's when I met him. Brightstone sponsored both of us to present to the National Association of Teachers of English."

"How much contact did you have after that?"

"I must say, I wondered why I was meeting him all the time in the hallways of Brightstone and Kiwi. At least, I had some expertise to share. I don't know what he offered but a good personality and sports background. Of course, there were continuing rumors about his college relationship with Greenwood, and that Greenwood was trying to put a lid on any loose talk about it."

"Do you think Greenwood might want to kill Blanchard to shut him up about this rumored relationship?"

"I don't think Greenwood would go that far; plus, Blanchard had to worry about his image if any of the rumors proved true."

"So how did Blanchard become secretary?"

"I don't want to be immodest, but I certainly had better qualifications for the job than Blanchard. Many said I should be the next secretary. But Blanchard was the golden boy for both Kiwi and Brightstone, with his good looks, athleticism, and personality. I thought he was a phony, constantly making sports references in his speeches."

"So you wanted to be secretary?" Tim's dislike of Riesling was increasing as the interview continued.

"Yes and no! I'm doing well here, but I think as secretary I could have saved the schools and all those minority kids. But Brightstone and Kiwi had poured money into the president's reelection campaign, and both companies wanted Blanchard to be secretary."

"According to our data, and I need to warn you again all government files are open to investigators, you make considerably more than the average college professor. In fact, your total income is higher than that of any college president. Last year you made $3.5 million before taxes."

"I'm a well-recognized scholar in my field, and I earn income from consulting." Riesling stood up and looked at a group of students playing Frisbee in the quad below. "I am well known as an expert on the Common Core, and many states seek my advice on implementation."

Glancing down at his papers, Tim asserted, "You also seemed to have earned money from consulting for the US Department of Education and, of course, Brightstone and Kiwi. Also, there are your earnings from stock holdings in both companies and the Common Core Fund."

"What can I say?" Riesling turned away from the window and looked directly at Tim. "I've never been interested in money or making a career. But others see me as talented. I view myself a selfless scholar in pursuit of truth."

"What about China?" Tim tried not to burst out laughing at the claim of selflessness. "Last year you made several trips to the Kiwi's Jinan plant. What was that about?"

"That's our big project on making a teacher robot. It is the only hope for American schools. In fact, I've been advocating in recent speeches to replace human teachers with robots. Robots are the best hope for poor and minority students."

"Do you think the Chinese might be involved in the poisoning or the charter-school bombing?"

"What a preposterous idea!" Riesling responded vehemently. "I have very strong and positive feelings about the Chinese struggle to improve the lot of their citizens. Some of my best friends are Chinese. I've always been treated with honor and graciousness on every visit. Their banquets are models of good hospitality, though I have a hard time with toasts and the heavy drinking."

"I see," Tim said, looking at one of the framed diplomas on the wall, "that you earned an honorary doctorate from Tsinghua University."

"I was very proud to receive that degree." Riesling smiled. "They're the best school in China. My book *The Technology of Learning* has been translated into Chinese and used in all major schools. I think China is beginning to understand that a robot is a better teacher than a human."

"According to an NSA report on China, you received the degree after Brightstone and Kiwi donated a large sum to Tsinghua."

"Those two companies are helping schools around the world. The donation added to the prestige of my degree. Since then I've been asked to lecture all over China, but I've declined because of the pollution. I worry it will shorten my life."

"Who do you think might have wanted to poison the secretary or bomb the school?" Tim glanced at his watch, wanting to catch the red-eye back to Cincinnati. He was also experiencing the unusual feeling of missing someone, namely, Felicia.

"I don't know, but there are many out there opposed to the Common Core. I get hate mail about the Common Core all the time from both left- and right-wing organizations. Every time I consult with state officials, the e-mails and snail mail flood in from anti-testing and anti–Common Core groups located in those states."

"We'll need to look at those messages," Tim said.

"I deleted and destroyed many of them. I can send what's left to you."

"Hm." Tim paused, thinking about the communications restrictions of Homeland Security. "I'll have someone contact you to come to your office to read them and take notes. Is there any particular group you're concerned about?"

"Stop Testing has been the most strident and threatening." Riesling suddenly paled. "Do you think my life is in danger?"

Sensing Riesling's fear, Tim decided to not let him off the hook. "You should be concerned, until we find the killer or killers. As an FBI agent, I am required to warn you of any personal danger. You should be very cautious in the future."

"I have to worry about poisoning," Riesling gasped. "Tomorrow I'm to talk to the National Council of Social Studies Teachers in Denver on the value of the Common Core for teaching patriotism. Should I have bodyguards or a food taster?"

"I can't advice you on any particular course of action," Tim said, relishing Riesling's discomfort. "Just be careful; there are terrorists out there. You might want to tell Horton University officials about your fears."

"I will check into bodyguards. I don't know about the university." Riesling was clearly nervous.

"Speaking of the Common Core and patriotism, I understand that Secretary Blanchard wanted the robots to teach the world about the value of free markets, democracy, and English. Is that true?"

"We're all patriots," Riesling said proudly. "We were all in agreement that the teaching robot would be important in spreading pro-American ideas around the world. Heaven knows this country doesn't have a good international image."

"Who's the 'we'?"

"Why, the heads of Kiwi and Brightstone, myself, and, of course, Blanchard," Riesling responded. "One of our comparative education professors claims that the teacher robot will launch a new chapter in the culture wars that is guaranteed to win the hearts and minds of the world's peoples."

Chapter 15

"There's money to be made helping poor kids," Tim said to Felicia over lunch the next day. He was still feeling groggy from the red-eye and was not relishing the thought of leaving for Washington for an evening meeting at Homeland Security on conservative suspects.

"That sounds terribly cynical Tim," Felicia frowned.

"This investigation is getting to me. I wish I could tell you about what I'm finding. It would raise your union hackles." He bit into his tuna sandwich. "Anything new about the union saving schools?"

"We met yesterday in Detroit with this secret group of superintendents. Sorry, I can't tell you their names. I don't think they would like being thrown into your investigation."

"Anything come out of the meeting?" Tim sat back and took a sip of his coffee.

"It's really difficult getting any media attention. The media doesn't seem to like printing stories supporting public schools. The privatization and technology people get all the space."

"My advice, after talking to this sleazeball Horton professor, is that you hire a good public relations firm with contacts to major media outlets. There's big money behind the push for privatization of schools."

Tim glanced at his watch, worrying about making the Washington flight. "Any more hate mail?"

"Union leaders are being bombarded by this racist stuff from that crazy Silvershirts and Whiteperson Association. One note talked vaguely about attacking union headquarters in Washington."

"If you have any of those messages, I'd like to take them to Washington this afternoon."

"I've collected some." Felicia gave him a thick folder. "Some of it is just plain vile."

"I've gotta get to the airport." Tim checked his watch again. "I'll be back tomorrow. Are you doing anything tomorrow evening?"

"Just waiting for you."

* * *

"It's strange, the number of bicycles on Washington streets these days," Tim commented, entering Homeland Security's safe room, where Eliot Spooner, Alan Olsen, and Floyd Henderson were already seated looking through a pile of documents. "It looks like old street photos of China before anyone could afford cars."

"Part of the new bike-sharing program," Alan replied. "There are rumors that all government employees are going to be required to ride bikes to work or take public transportation. All government parking facilities will be shut. It's supposed to end traffic congestion and pollution."

"This is another step back to the Dark Ages," Eliot commented. "First we end electronic communications and now cars."

"As I see it," Floyd said, "technology is self-destructing. Cars were the modern transportation dream, but traffic and pollution killed them, and we have to return to more-primitive forms, like bicycles and walking. Bike sharing sounds like a reform idea of the 1890s."

"Yes, credit cards were to make it easier to spend," Eliot added. "Fraud is driving the cards out of people's wallets, and they're returning to cash."

"I wonder when this devolution of technology will end," Eliot continued. "I was joking with my wife that they'll make us give up dishwashers because of energy costs and water pollution. We'll have to spend every evening washing and drying dishes together with biodegradable soap. I remember my mom complaining that her mother made her wash dishes every night."

"Let's get to the task at hand," Alan interrupted the conversation. "Tim, what have you found out since the last meeting?"

Tim opened his new briefcase, which he was forced to buy when he could no longer carry his laptop or tablet. "Here are some threatening messages being sent to the teachers union by a group called the Silvershirts and Whiteperson Association."

"We've been following that group for years, since members dragged a black man in Texas behind a pickup," Eliot told them. "Of course, the man died, and the perpetrators were arrested. But, given small-town Texas, a jury found them not guilty. They are an extremely violent group."

"Do you think they would be interested in poisoning the secretary and bombing the school?" Alan asked.

"Some of its members are certainly capable," Eliot replied, "but I don't know if they're that upset about school issues. What do their letters indicate?"

"Well," Tim said, opening the folder he removed from his briefcase, "they accuse the union and school-people in general of being more interested in educating black kids than white kids. Some of their more racist comments suggest that black students should be educated in zoos."

"That's the type of racism in these other groups." Floyd opened a large manila folder. "First, I want to say"—Floyd looked at each person in the safe room—"after investigating these groups, I've renewed my membership in the NAACP and the Southern Poverty Law Center. This stuff scares the shit out of my black body. I hope all of you appreciate how difficult it is as a black man to contain my anger toward these groups."

Laying a couple of documents on the conference table, Floyd continued. "Similar statements are coming from the Utah Association of Nordic People, the Aryan Club of Georgia, the Alabama League for Promoting White People, and the National Association for the Advancement of White People. There is another national group promoting what it calls the 'Glories of the Nazi Age.' All these groups have been conducting hate campaigns against federal involvement in schools and racial integration. The National Association for the Advancement of White People has been distributing a booklet justifying resegregation of public schools."

"Besides racial issues, do these groups have any other education concerns?" Alan asked.

"The racism of these groups," Floyd explained, "blankets issues of evolution, abstinence education, school prayer, patriotic education, and, of course, the federal government."

"Evolution—how did that get on their agenda?" Eliot wondered.

"Their literature argues that teaching evolution is a brainwashing method for teaching equality of the races. They deny that white and black people could have shared a common ancestor."

"But according to Congressman Bollinger," Tim interjected, "Secretary Blanchard wasn't too keen on evolution and wanted things like intelligent design taught. Evolution wouldn't be a reason for killing him."

"These groups aren't exactly rational. Blanchard was vilified in their literature as a representative of federal intervention to create racial equality," Floyd reported. "Also, their literature both criticizes and supports expansion of charter schools."

"Why would they support charter schools?" Alan asked.

"They believe charter schools can be used to resegregate schools. As far as I can tell from their literature, they might not have opposed the Booker T. Washington Charter School in Cincinnati, because all the students were black—that is, it was a segregated school."

"Are charters resulting in segregation?" Tim asked.

"Analyzing the data, charters in some parts of the country are a new form of racial segregation," Floyd answered. "However, the National Association for the Advancement of White People wants charter laws changed to allow for white-only schools and the teaching of white-supremacy doctrines. As they point out, national charter school chains like the Booker T. Washington schools appear to recruit only black students."

"What about abstinence education? Why would these Nazis be concerned?" Alan asked.

"One of the Silvershirts and Whiteperson Association's letters to the union," Tim explained, "called for abstinence education in all schools serving minorities while advocating— and this is hard to believe—love-ins in white schools. In addition to abstinence education, they want to provide free sterilization to male and female students in all minority schools. They want white kids to have more children and minority kids to stop, to use their words, breeding."

"So," Alan summarized, "these neo-Nazi groups are capable of violence and demonstrate an extreme dislike for federal education policies. There might be reasons for suspecting them of killing the secretary, but they might not have been interested in bombing the charter school. We should keep these groups on our suspect list. What about any other right-wing groups?"

"There are Christian groups, particularly the Jesus Coalition, which has been leading campaigns for school prayer, Bible reading, and abstinence education," Eliot explained. "And, like some of the Nazi groups, they cling to the notion of American exceptionalism."

"What's American exceptionalism?" asked Floyd.

"It's a belief that God has chosen the United States to spread Christianity and freedom around the world," Eliot answered. "Of course, this is a limited concept of freedom, since these groups are not libertines. For them, freedom means the right to choose to be Christian, to shop, and to compete in a free market."

"Are they violent? Should we keep them on the list?" Alan asked.

"There have been different sorts of violence. There was a Florida minister who caused international riots by a public burning of the Koran. And there are reports from around the country of local branches of the Jesus Crusade burning mosques and abortion clinics. Some have been linked to the shooting of abortion doctors."

"Have they threatened any educators or schools?" Tim asked.

"A Texas group called Christians for the American Way," Eliot answered, "had a public burning of the state-adopted history texts and threw eggs at the state education commissioner. They claim the books were pro-Islamic, because they didn't discuss the 1805 American war against Barbary Coast pirates."

"Barbary Coast pirates—I guess I don't know my American history," Floyd responded.

"They claim it was the first war against Islamic terrorism and want a prominent place for it in US history books," Eliot replied. "The Marine Corps hymn refers to the war as the shores of Tripoli." Eliot sang the opening lines of the Marine Corps hymn:

From the Halls of Montezuma,
To the shores of Tripoli;
We fight our country's battles
In the air, on land, and sea.

"They've picketed Texas's Brightstone Testing Center," Eliot continued, "demanding more test questions about the Tripoli campaign and for a greater emphasis on America's role in spreading Christianity and democracy. The demonstrators scuffled with police when they tried to block an armored truck full of tests from entering the center. Three police ended up in the hospital. This test center's seen a lot of activity. You will recall that the Stop Test group poured acid on answer sheets there."

"We can add Christians for the American Way to our list of possible terrorists." Alan wrote down on his paper pad.

"The Church of Jesus Christ Christian-Aryan Nations, or, as it is also known as, Aryan Nations Knights of the Ku Klux Klan, is another group to consider," Eliot looked down at his notes. "Based in Converse,

Louisiana, they bill themselves as 'The World's Premier Christian Identity Church Organization.' Their stated goal is," Eliot read, "'a united racial convocation to establish a national and international Aryan solidarity of purpose for the existence, sustenance and reproduction of our Race.'"

"This goal," Eliot continues, "fits other rightist complaints that abstinence education should not target white kids but that it should be part of a non-reproduction education program for minorities."

"I hardly need to ask, given the gruesome history of the Klan, whether there is any current suggestion of violence?" asked Owen.

"You might consider the following statement as lending itself to militancy." Eliot read: "THEREFORE: WE, A REMNANT OF OUR RACIAL ARYAN NATION, who have not and will not bow the knee to the destroyer, do hereby seek a convocation, a Congress to meet in solemn assembly to HOIST A STANDARD and commence a great Aryan Racial Regeneration, to separate ourselves individually and nationally from laboring for that which destroys US."

"I'm not sure what that means for education," Tim commented.

"I found a flyer for the organization's biker rally last year in Illinois," Eliot continued. "It advertises a fund-raiser, bike wash, raffle, cookout, and, it claims, according to this flyer, 'All Proceeds go to Benefit the Education Outreach Program of the Church of Jesus Christ Christian.' The flyer shows three white children reading a book with the captions 'Children—They're Our Future—Preserve Them' and 'We Must Secure the Existence of Our People and a Future for Our Children.'"

"The most troubling is the Aryan Nations Skinhead Division of the Klan," Eliot added.

"Skinhead Division!" Floyd exclaimed. "I thought the Klan was finished years ago. But I did check social media, text messages, and e-mails in Cincinnati and Ohio and found many discussions and hits on the Klan website."

"The Skinheads represent a problem," Eliot replied. "We've identified some Cincinnati high-school students as members. The Skinheads suggest possibilities of violence in their statement of principles." Eliot read from a letter sent out by the Aryan Nations Skinhead Division: "'The true soldiers stick around and endure the hardships that are thrust upon us by a society that seeks to suppress our message because they desire to destroy our people.... Struggle is deep in the blood of our Aryan race.... Are you up to the challenge and ready for the fight that must be waged?'"

"What about education?" Tim asked. "I know the Skinheads recruit in schools. And I know the Klan has strongly opposed school integration."

"They have an educational outreach program," Eliot answered. "Probably the most popular are their cartoon books." Eliot pulled some from his file. "As you can see, these four educational cartoon books have provocative titles like, *The Adventures of Whiteman, White Power Comes to Midvale, Aryanman Battles the Bestial Hordes,* and *National Socialist Liberation Front Underground Comics.* These cartoon books are used to recruit high-school students."

"Christ," commented Olson. "If there are Skinheads in Cincinnati, then it is always in the realm of possibilities that they would bomb a black charter school."

"I found from my Klan survey in Ohio," Floyd informed them, "that *White Power Comes to Midvale* is widely discussed and distributed among white Cincinnati high-school students. It has been a very effective recruiting tool."

"The cartoon is worth examining." Eliot held up a copy and began summarizing it. "The first panel shows a black student holding a white student by his shirt and commanding, 'C'mon Whitey.... It's either yo' lunch money or yo' teeth." Three panels later Eric Thompson, a white student new to the school, intervenes to protect the other white student and shoves a book into a black attacker's face saying, 'Pardon me, nigger, this is a school, I have something for you—a little book learning.' Then Eric punches the black student in the face, saying, 'Hope I'm not violating your civil rights, Hottentot.' Eventually the school principal, drawn as a cartoon Jewish stereotype and named Mr. Cohen, intervenes and scolds Eric and the other white student for being angry. Cohen tells them that 'underprivileged ghetto youth' need money and that the Constitution says we are all equal."

"Let me understand," a horrified-looking Tim said. "This comic is popular among Cincinnati white youth."

"Yes, and it gets worse," Eliot continued. "After the principal argues that the Constitution guarantees equality, Eric responds, 'The Constitution only says Negroes are three-fifths of a free white man." The principal dismisses him, saying, 'So who cares about these ignorant rednecks.' After a discussion lasting several panels about the meaning of equality, Eric says to the principal, 'I noticed you let the niggers wear Black Power T-shirts, so—' and Eric rips open his top shirt to reveal a T-shirt with a swastika and the words 'White Power.' In the final panels, Eric beats up black students, shouting, 'You're forgetting one thing, jigaboo! A National Socialist isn't fighting for just himself but for the future of his race.'"

"Are you sure," Tim asked, "that this comic is popular in Cincinnati?"

"It's widely cited on Facebook by Cincinnati students, and my investigators have read many e-mails and text messages either supporting—we assume these are white students—or vilifying the comic," Floyd said. "I'm surprised there hasn't been a race riot over the comic."

"Have you identified the skinheads responsible for promoting it?" Tim asked.

Floyd handed him a list of names and addresses.

"It's getting late, and we can continue in the morning," Alan announced. "We need to draft a list of suspects and prioritize it. Agent Geary, you should plan to leave tomorrow afternoon for Cincinnati."

Chapter 16

The knocking got louder and louder as Carl Grinder stumbled out of bed at seven in the morning and headed to his apartment door. Since the bombing Carl relished sleeping until Cherry had to get up for the 11:00 a.m. opening of the National Underground Railroad Freedom Center.

"We want our money," Blanch Cooper and Eric Somers shouted in unison as Grinder opened the door.

"I told you I'm waiting for money," Carl snapped back, clearly irritated by the early morning visit. "I've met with you several times about this. The state's delaying the charter-school money, since we're no longer operational."

"You seem to have plenty." Eric looked enviously through the door at the apartment's rich furnishing.

"We traced you on the web, and your family is wealthy; plus, you made millions investing." Blanch pushed her way into the apartment.

Awakened by the noise, Cherry joined them, expressing annoyance at the visit. "What are you doing, barging into our apartment at this time of the morning? Please leave."

"We're not leaving until we get paid," Eric said firmly. "I'm going to lose my home, and Blanch has kids to feed. You owe us money."

"FBI agent Geary told us you were rich," Blanch added. "You can afford to pay us out of your own pocket. I've cleaned out my savings. You promised to pay."

"You've been talking to the FBI about me?" Carl looked surprised. "Why would you do that?"

"Haven't you paid them?" Cherry turned to Carl. "You told me you were taking care of them."

"Why'd you see the FBI?" Carl asked anxiously, now fully awake.

"They'll tell you. Geary says he's going to look more closely at you and the bombing," Eric replied. "Now we just want our pay."

"What did you tell them?" Carl was now clearly alarmed, wondering what these two teachers reported.

"Why don't you just write them a check, and let's get some more rest?" ordered Cherry. "They've got to live."

"It's not that easy." Carl paused, not wanting to explain their financial situation in front of the teachers. "Marvin and Abe say to wait until they can send money from their charter-school fund and for the state charter-school funds."

"The state's not going to pay with the school closed," Blanch snapped, heading into the Grinder's living room.

"We didn't invite you in," Cherry called after her.

"We didn't asked to be bombed out of our salaries," Eric responded, following Blanch and sitting down on the Grinder's leather sofa. "We'll leave when we're paid. You rich people don't know what's it like to lose your wife and kids and now the house. The FBI's going to find out about you two."

"Jesus, Carl, just pay them." Cherry headed to the kitchen to make coffee. "And what's this about the FBI?"

"Yes, what is this about the FBI? What did you tell them?" Carl was feeling nervous about their FBI references. He wondered if it was about his financial problems.

"They know who did the bombing. You can't hide. We're not leaving until we're paid," Blanch said. "If you go to jail, then for sure we won't get paid. I've kids to feed."

"What's this about you going to jail?" Cherry came hurrying out of the kitchen on hearing Blanch's words.

"I don't know what they're talking about." Carl sat down in a chair opposite the two teachers. "What do you mean I'm going to jail?"

"You'll see," said Blanch. "You can't hide forever. Now pay what the school owes us. We're not leaving until we get the money."

"I still don't understand the jail issue." Cherry looked at her husband in dismay. "Just write them a check, and get them out of here."

"I don't know the amount, with taxes and health insurance deductions." Carl's mind was racing, trying to figure how to shut them up. He was worried about jail and the FBI.

"Here's our pay stubs." Eric handed them to Carl. "Just write a check for the net amount. We don't trust you Wall Street types, always taking money from people like us."

Also, Eric thought, I especially don't trust blacks.

"I can't do this," Carl responded.

"I don't know what's going, on but I'll write them checks." Cherry went over to Eric and plucked the pay stubs out his hand and headed into the room they used as a common office.

"I told you they both had money," Blanch said to Eric. "These rich people look down on us." Secretly, Blanch wanted to say rich blacks just wanted to lord it over poor whites.

Cherry returned with two checks for the teachers. "Just take these and leave. I understand your financial concerns, but if you come again. I will call the police."

"The police'll get you soon enough," Eric called back over his shoulder as they left.

"What's this about the police and jail?" Cherry said as she closed the apartment door.

"I don't know," Carl answered.

"What'd you mean, you don't know? Why didn't you just write them a check? They certainly need it after the bombing."

"It's not that simple," Carl answered. "I'm a little short of funds, and I hope your checks don't bounce."

"What do you mean, my checks bouncing? What haven't you been telling me about?"

"There've been problems with the Common Core Fund. I put my money into it because of the teacher robot. It's going to make a fortune with sales around the world. Remember one reason I took the principal job was to be the first to use it."

"You're saying you've lost your money because of the teacher robot. What about mine? How did my money get involved?"

"I had to dip into your accounts to cover some losses in the fund. You'll get it all back when we join the super-rich and become world-famous because of the robot."

"You dipped into my money without telling me. How could you? Didn't that robot fail! You mean we're broke," Cherry yelled at him, picking up a vase and hurling it at his head.

"We'll be okay; they're testing the robot again soon. Everyone knows it'll make a fortune."

"You still haven't explained jail. Will I be going to jail?"

"We're not going to jail. I think they were referring to the financial problems Elizabeth Factor is having at the Common Core Fund. We're not responsible for any legal problems faced by the fund."

"Legal problems! What kind of legal problems?" Cherry sat down and started crying. "I can't believe you put your money and mine, I guess, into an investment fund with legal problems. What did you learn all those years on Wall Street?"

"This wasn't supposed to happen; who knew that a kid's vomit would screw this all up. We were to just come to Cincinnati and show the world that a robot was a better teacher than humans."

"What was all this bullshit you told me back in New York about giving up making money and saving poor kids?" Cherry pushed Carl's hand away as he tried to comfort her.

"I couldn't tell you everything."

"What do you mean, you couldn't tell me everything?" Cherry stood, looking like she wanted to hit Carl. "Since when do we keep secrets from each other?"

"I was sworn to secrecy by the CIA."

"The CIA—what've they got to do with us coming to Cincinnati?"

"They approached me in New York about the teacher robot project. They told me I couldn't discuss it with anyone, including you." Carl stared at the floor, thinking how crazy this must sound to Cherry.

"The CIA is planning to use the robot as part of a major cultural offensive against the Chinese," Carl explained. "When they told me, I realized I could make a lot of money by piggybacking on the CIA plans."

"So you invested all our money," Cherry said, weeping, "because of some CIA plan, and now we're broke, because some Chinese kid vomited, and you're going to be arrested."

"I'm not going to be arrested. I don't know what those teachers were talking about. And we'll get our money back when Kiwi finishes the next robot demonstration."

"So what're we going to live on? We can't afford this apartment on my salary."

"We paid a yearly lease, so we don't have to move." Carl said. "And, yes we've got to live on your salary until the robot gets sold."

"What about your friends Marvin Goldman and Abe Stein? Can't they pay you and your teachers? They've got plenty of money."

"They also put their money in the Common Core Fund. Remember, we all thought, with the CIA involved, this was a sure thing. Plus, anyone knows a robot can teach better than a human."

Outside the Grinders' apartment building, Blanch and Eric looked at their checks and congratulated each other for planning to confront the principal in his apartment early in the morning.

"Did you see that expensive furniture? These uppity blacks take any opportunity to lord it over us." Blanch looked up at the Grinders' apartment windows. "They can afford Mt. Adams, while I have to worry about feeding my kids."

"They'll be singing a different tune when the FBI arrests them for the bombing." Eric said. "All this talk about equality is just a means of stealing from whites to give to lazy blacks."

"I think I saw some Chinese stuff on their mantel. I bet he brought it back with him after they planned the bombing." Blanch started walking in direction of a bank machine she'd seen when they'd driven to the apartment building. "I've got to deposit this right away."

"Same here." Eric went with her.

"All this stuff about helping blacks," Blanch continued. "What about us whites? We're just getting poor paying taxes to give more money to them."

"The Civil War was just an excuse for blacks to use the government to rob whites," Eric said angrily. "All they talk about is equality and giving more money to black kids. White kids are losing out in school."

"I know," Blanch agreed. "I wouldn't have taken that job if I could have taught white kids. But the charter was the only place hiring."

"The only good thing," Eric said, "was that it was all black. Segregation is better for them; keeps them with their own."

"Every time I hear the word 'equality,'" Blanch said, slipping her debit card into the ATM, "I want to scream. 'Equality' is just another word for stealing from whites. We could see how much Grinder believed in equality, when he had us changing test scores."

As Blanch and Eric were depositing their checks in Mt. Adams's ATM, Secretary Olsen passed out his list of suspects to the investigative team meeting in Homeland Security's safe room. "Here's my list; I've divided suspects into primary and secondary."

"There are some other possibilities we didn't discuss yesterday," Eliot said, looking at his notes. "There are Tea Party and Libertarian groups strongly opposed to federal intervention in school. Also, there are the teachers unions who have been fighting tooth and nail against charter schools."

"What have you got on these groups?" Alan asked Floyd Henderson, counting on his team having already looked at the data on these groups.

"We've been monitoring the e-mail, text messages, and social media of the teacher union leaders. We haven't found anything that might suggest being involved in the poisoning or bombing."

"What about the Tea Party? They've been raising a ruckus about all federal programs and particularly federal support of the Common Core Standards," Tim asked.

"They're clean too," Floyd responded. "We've been reading all Tea Party communications since their congressional representatives shut down the government by not passing a budget. Last year, our office tagged the effort to close the government as a danger to national security."

"What!" Tim was surprised. "You've been reading their communications. They're a political group. If the Republican Party finds out, we're going to face a lot of criticism.

Ignoring Tim, Floyd continued, "The Libertarian Party's communications are clean, but there is a libertarian group in California called LiberAnarcho. It's a Mexican group composed of illegals advocating open immigration and the abolishment of the government. Some members have communicated with each other about taking violent action against all governments. We've identified them and tracked their movements through their cell phones. While they should be considered suspects, I tend to think they are not involved, because little of their communication has anything to do with schools, and none refers to the Secretary of Education."

"What do you recommend?" Alan asked.

"We can add them to your list of secondary suspects, though we might want to put LiberAnarchos in the primary list if we find communications that could be interpreted as threatening schools. At this point, they're primarily interested in opening the border with Mexico to allow for a free exchange of citizens."

"Okay, let's discuss my list. You'll note I've put China in a separate category, because it involves the CIA and the State Department. The Chinese government does have reasons for poisoning the secretary because of the culture wars and the teacher robot."

"I want to mention that two teachers from the bombed charter school came to see me, claiming the principal was involved with the Chinese and worked with them to commit the bombing," Tim said. "Their suspicions are based on a box they saw in the school's storage room with Chinese characters and stamps. The principal was supposed to demonstrate the teacher robot, and the box might have something to do with that."

"What are the teachers' names?" Floyd asked. "I'll have my team find out about them."

"They seemed a little kooky but not dangerous," Tim said. "The male is named Eric Somers; and the female, Blanch Cooper."

"Also in a special category are Brightstone, Kiwi, and the Common Core Fund. These two companies and the investment firm have connections with China, the Department of Education, the Booker T. Washington Charter Schools, and a web of other people. There is a possibility that someone in this web did the poisoning and bombing. But we still don't have a motive."

"The primary domestic suspects, based on our discussions, data, and past violent actions," Alan continued, "are Hug Our Trees, No More Growth, Stop Testing, Silvershirts and Whiteperson Association, and the Skinhead Division of the Church of Jesus Christian-Aryan Nations. My secondary suspect list includes teachers unions, Rescue Our Schools, the Jesus Crusade, and LiberAnarcho."

"Can you add any other group or person?" Alan asked.

"Boss, this looks complete at this time," Tim said. "I think there might be something in this Brightstone, Kiwi, Common Core Fund, and China web. There's something not quite right. Also, this web connects directly with the culture wars."

"Floyd," Olson ordered, "I want you to go over all the data we have on these three companies and work with the CIA on the China connections."

Turning to Tim, Alan instructed, "I think Stop Testing is a major suspect. They've been violent and were opposed to Secretary Blanchard, and they hate charter schools. I'd like you to go to Philadelphia tomorrow and personally talk to them. Also, I would like you to continue your investigation of all the work being done on the teacher robot."

"Speaking of the teacher robot," Eliot said, "a courier brought back a letter from our new China spy that they're planning another teacher-robot demonstration tomorrow."

"From the data we have on the Common Core Fund, if this demonstration fails, the whole fund may sink, taking many people with it," Floyd informed them.

Chapter 17

They crammed into the small room behind the one-way glass looking into a classroom of twenty students receiving instructions from Sally2, the reprogrammed teacher robot. Brightstone's President John Greenwood, its Vice President for Marketing Marty Cohn, and the President of the Brightstone Foundation Ruben Bush were present, as were Kiwi's President Jack Phillipson and his wife and president of Phillipson Foundation, Mary Phillipson. Sitting next to them in the front row, facing the one-way glass, was a very nervous Elizabeth Factor, president of the Common Core Fund. Behind them sat Kiwi's Vice President of School Technologies Gordon Brader, the Vice President of Robotic Teaching Bert Robinson, and Jennifer Robinson, vice president of robotic emotions.

Sitting along the wall were three staff members from the US embassy, two of whom were from the CIA. Sitting along the opposite wall was a representative from the Chinese government's Hanban office and one from the Ministry of State Security.

Huddled in back of the room around a table was the Communist Party's Technology Planning Team (TPT) talking loudly in Chinese, knowing the Westerners couldn't understand them. Even Bert and

Jennifer, after several years at the Jinan plant, couldn't understand the language, since everyone insisted on speaking English with them.

"Liao Yiwu," Li Luan lowered his voice, whispering to the man in charge of programming, "are you sure there will be no evidence of the virus or Confucian chip during this demonstration?"

"There will be no evidence of their existence," Liao assured Luan. "They are activated six months after the robots are first booted up. Sally2 will be powered off after this demonstration, for final reworking."

"Please note," whispered TPT's public relations expert Tan Zuoren into Luan's ear, "there are two CIA agents along with one high-ranking official from the Hanban and an officer from the Ministry of State Security. I'm sure the CIA agents know Chinese so we should guard our words."

"She looks pretty fashionable," Mary Phillipson said to her husband about Sally2. "I like her dress and shirt."

"Supposedly, Li Luan ordered Ralph Lauren clothes from his cousin Wang Bing," John replied.

"Luan," John called to him in the back of the room. "Are those the clothes from your cousin?"

"Yes," Luan answered proudly in English, so that everyone could hear. "Sally2 is wearing an antique sage beaded angora crewneck and a matching silk mousseline skirt. Wang Bing took the design directly from a Ralph Lauren catalogue. He flew to Jinan to measure Sally2 to get the clothes right."

On the other side of the one-way glass, Sally2 was moving slowly down the aisle between two rows of ten students each, giving instructions for a geometry lesson on the Pythagorean theorem. Sally2's voice simulated a recording of an Iowa female schoolteacher. Other English-speaking voices could be substituted to match regional accents. Kiwi had sent out teams to places such as India, Nigeria, and Australia to record teachers speaking English.

"Looks okay so far," Jennifer commented to Bert, who was perspiring, worried about Sally2's failing. His boss Jack Phillipson threatened to fire him if there was another screw-up.

"I hope that last-minute adjustment in its software will block the virus we detected in the program," Bert said softly. "There was something weird going on when we used the National Security Agency's new virus scanner yesterday. The old Kiwi scanner didn't detect anything. The NSA insisted we use their new virus program, which can identify newer Chinese viruses. But we didn't get it until two days ago."

"What did it find?"

"There's a virus in Sally2's software, but it doesn't seem to be active. Plus, it found some kind of strange chip in the motherboard."

Sally2 stopped next to a student working on a computer tablet that directly communicated with the robot. The room grew quiet as they watched the robot bend over and point at the tablet, saying, "The proof is based on the proportionality of the sides of two similar triangles; that is, upon the fact that the ratio of any two corresponding sides of similar triangles is the same, regardless of the size of the triangles."

"That sounds too formal," Jack Phillipson turned around and said to Bert. "We should have more ordinary language. I'm not sure how many sixth-graders are going to understand that explanation."

"It's directly from one of our sixth-grade texts," John Greenwood said, overhearing the discussion. "Also, it is exactly what's written in our math tests. The lesson is good preparation for passing."

"We've got software that'll adapt those sentences to local speech patterns of children in the nations using the robot," Bert explained. "Sally2's speech is now formal, since it's quoting Brightstone's texts."

The room gasped as Sally2 straightened up with its arm almost hitting the student. "Sorry," Sally2 said.

"There are sensors all over Sally2's structure which set off alarms when it is too close to a student," Jennifer explained to Kiwi's president. "We eliminated the kissing."

"The Chinese were asking for empathy," Jack replied. "Will the robot feel hurt if it did hit the student?"

"Empathy is impossible. And even if we could, the Chinese agree that it might be dangerous and cause teacher robots to unite," Jennifer replied. "Sally2 automatically says 'sorry' if it's too close to a student. That way it sounds caring."

Suddenly Sally2's head lit up in alternating green, red, and blue flashing colors, and smiley faces appeared on its cheeks and forehead. Gold stars looked like they were flowing down its simulated throat, accompanied by what sounded like coins clanking together. Sally2 wheeled swiftly over to a student's desk, and a small amount of M&Ms came out of its palm.

"That's our reinforcement and praise," Jennifer said loudly, so all could hear. "That student was the first to prove the theorem."

"Sounds like she won the jackpot," Greenwood commented.

"Actually," Jennifer said, very proud of this reinforcing display, "we recorded slot machines in Macao, Singapore, and Las Vegas. Those are the actual sounds made by slots when they pay out."

Sally2, after piling candy on the student's desk, wheeled to the front of the class, and all the brightly flashing colors, smiley faces, and sounds ended. Sally2 announced, "It is time for our English lesson. Please click on the English icon on your tablet and go to sixth grade."

One student raised his hand, and Sally2 recognized the hand by pointing a laser beam at it. "What do you need, Shi Tao?" Sally said.

"We built this recognition into Sally2's software. It immediately recognizes a raised hand and identifies the student," Bert explained to the group.

The student, a scrawny boy, said in Chinese, "I have to go to the bathroom."

"Shi Tao, you can go to the bathroom. Take the electronic pass."

"Please notice," Bert said, standing up so that all could hear him. "Sally2 has voice and visual recognition. It can immediately identify a student, and it can immediately interpret any language and the actual meaning of the words."

"Can it tell if the student is lying? What happens if this kid just wants to skip out of school?" asked Ken Russell, one of the CIA agents. "I used to get a bathroom pass to meet my girlfriend by our lockers."

"The electronic pass monitors and records the student's actions. With its GPS it can determine if the student is going to the boy's room. Any deviation from the route will automatically signal Sally2," explained Bert.

"What happens if students smoke in the bathroom or do other things?" Russell asked.

"The electronic pass has a scent detector that sets off an alarm if the student lights up. Our major problem we discovered were boys masturbating in the stalls. If the electronic pass detects the smell of semen, a message is sent to Sally2."

"I think my agency would find this useful," CIA Agent Russell blurted out.

"Also, we could use it," said Bao Tong of the Ministry of State Security.

"What about sending the kid to the principal's office or the library?" Jack asked.

"The GPS monitors the student's path through the school; plus, it's visual and scent-recognition systems can identify a principal's office or the library. The visuals and smells of all staff members and rooms are stored in the teaching robot," Bert explained.

"We are going to practice your oral understanding of English," Sally2 said to the class. "Please type into your tablets as best you can the following quote from the great economist Milton Friedman. Don't worry about mistakes. I will immediately assess your texts and send back corrections and hints for better understanding oral English."

Sally2 slowly said to the class as they tried to type the quote into their tablets: "'The only way that has ever been discovered to have a lot of people cooperate together voluntarily is through the free market. And that's why it's so essential to preserving individual freedom.'"

"Secretary Blanchard would have loved that quote," Greenwood whispered to the president of the Brightstone Foundation, Reuben Bush. "We might want to use it on the Brightstone Foundation's flyers."

"See what I mean?" Luan said softly to his assistant Wang Lin. "Sally2 is programmed to spread reactionary capitalist ideas around the world."

After completing work on the Friedman quote and sending corrections and suggestions to each student, Sally2 read another quote, this time from American politician Jack Kemp: "'There's no limit to what free men and free women in a free market with free enterprise can accomplish when people are free to follow their dream.'"

"Oh my God," Bert shouted out as Sally 2 began to spin in place with its head displaying flashing colors and its sound system emitting noises of jackpots winnings.

The spinning, flashing colors, and sounds came to an abrupt end, and Sally2's head glowed red as it announced, "The next quote is from our beloved Mao Zedong."

Sally2, much to the shock of those watching through the one-way glass, said, with the first line spoken in English and the second in Chinese, "'Communism is not love. Communism is a hammer which we use to crush the enemy.'"

Good Lord, CIA Agent Russell thought to himself, this robot is an instrument of Chinese aggression and imperialism.

The Hanban representative Liao Yiwu jumped out of his chair, shouting, "We can't let this robot say that! We cannot operate Confucian Institutes with this message going around the world. We're in a culture war, not an arms war."

Then everyone stared as Sally2 spun around and faced the confused students with an American flag pulsating on its forehead. "Please, type into your tablets the following quote from the great economist Milton Friedman: "'The historical debate is over. The answer is free-market capitalism.'"

"What's going on?" Jennifer whispered to her husband. "I thought the software was okay."

Ready to break down crying, Bert worried, "It could be that virus and the end of my career."

Sally2 spun around again, with its face now looking like an ancient drawing of Confucius, and said in Chinese, "Please, type into your tablets the following quote from the world's greatest philosopher, Confucius: 'In a country well governed, poverty is something to be ashamed of. In a country badly governed, wealth is something to be ashamed of.'"

"What was that quote?" John asked Vice President for Marketing Marty Cohn. "Is it on any of our tests?"

"That is a direct attack on America," CIA Agent Russell answered, overhearing John's question. Russell translated the quote, enraging the Americans in the room.

"Type into your computer tablets," Sally2 continued, without giving time for the students to react to the last Confucian quote, "This statement by our great philosopher Confucius: 'If there were an honorable way to get rich, I'd do it, even if it meant being a stooge standing around with a whip. But there isn't an honorable way, so I just do what I like.'"

"Enough of this!" Russell jumped up, translating the quote for the group. "This is clearly anti-American and anti-capitalist."

Pointing his finger at the president of Kiwi, Russell accused him, "Jack, you should be aware that you and Kiwi will be considered an enemy of America and a national security threat if this robot is sold around the world."

Luan whispered to Yiwu, "I thought the Confucius chip would take six months to activate. What's happened?"

"I don't know, unless they recently did some kind of work on the motherboard," Yiwu replied. "I heard them mention when I was in Jinan yesterday something about a new American virus scanner."

Suddenly the room went silent, then the spectators gasped, as Sally2's head began to spin with alternating Chinese and American flags flashing on its forehead. As the head spun faster and faster, Sally2 began to sing alternating lines of the Chinese and American national anthems:

Arise! All those who don't want to be slaves!

O say can you see, by the dawn's early light,

Let our flesh and blood forge our new Great Wall!

What so proudly we hailed at the twilight's last gleaming,
As the Chinese people have arrived at their most perilous time.
Whose broad stripes and bright stars through the perilous fight,
Every person is forced to expel his very last roar."

Sally2's head spun off its body as it reached the lines of the Chinese anthem: "Arise! Arise! Arise! Our million hearts beating as one." The heavy, metal head hit two students in the front row, leaving them with severe concussions and broken facial bones. Their blood splattered against the one-way glass.

The observers sat stunned, watching the blood trickle down the glass.

Elizabeth Factor jumped up and ran to the exit, shouting she was ruined. She emerged from the building near Wangfujing and ran in the direction of Tiananmen Square. The pollution was so thick that she was quickly gasping for air. Someone had told her that running in Beijing could kill you. With that in mind, she ran hard pass Tiananmen, and, as the smog accumulated in her lungs and deprived her of oxygen, she collapsed at the entrance to the Communist compound Zhongnanhai. Her head hit the concrete curb, hastening her death.

Chapter 18

"I can't believe this," Carl Grinder said to himself over his morning coffee, as he looked at headline of a *New York Times* front-page article: "California Prisoners Riot Over the Common Core."

It was the same day as Sally2's ill-fated demonstration, with Beijing being twelve hours ahead of Cincinnati. Because of a twelve-hour time-zone difference between Beijing and New York, the paper was able to include before going to press a short article about Elizabeth Factor's death at the gates of the Communist Chinese compound.

"Cherry," he called into the kitchen, where his wife was finishing her breakfast before heading to work, "can you believe that prisoners have shut down a California prison over the Common Core State Standards?"

"What?" Cherry yelled from the kitchen, "A prison riot, but why?"

"Some prisoners at Chico State Prison were taking courses for their GED when California started the new Common Core tests," he called into the kitchen. "It says here that since their courses were not based on the Common Core, they weren't prepared for the exams. Most failed, causing the riot."

"I'm sure no one thought of prison riots because of tests." Cherry waved good-bye to Carl as she left for the Freedom Center. She had stopped kissing him good-bye after learning about him taking her money.

"Have a good day." Carl waved back. "There also appear to be prison gangs involved."

"Prison gangs?" Cherry paused as she opened the apartment door.

"This article says that prison gang members taking GED courses were using outside gang members to organize cheating services."

"That sounds like a long story. You can tell me about it later." Cherry left.

Carl shook his head as he read about the California prison gangs Nuestra Familia, Aryan Brotherhood, and Black Guerrilla Family organizing cheating services for state exams. Apparently, gang members in prison sought illegal help to pass the GED and other tests. They quickly learned that these services could be profitable if offered outside of prison.

Carl went into the kitchen to fill his cup and noticed that Cherry had left a mess. With the school and money gone, they could no longer afford a housekeeper to clean up.

"This is unbelievable," Carl said out loud, returning to the news article and reading:

Each gang offers cheating services to parents. The Aryan Brotherhood helps poor white kids pass tests, and the Nuestra Family does the same for Mexican American families, and the Black Guerrilla Family for black kids. The gangs, in one of the few times they cooperated, hijacked a convoy of Brightstone armored trucks carrying state tests. They sold copies of the tests to parents, with answers supplied by college students who were paid with drugs. Minority test scores in California rose as gangs became more involved in the shady side of the testing industry.

Carl sat back, dreaming about organizing cheating services to replenish the family coffers. It's not much different than other investments I've made, he thought. I always felt guilty about my oil investments, with those companies cheating and lying while causing war and destroying the environment.

He continued reading the article about how the riots started when the cheating services inside and outside California prisons were disrupted by the introduction of new Common Core based tests. Outside members of the Nuestra Familia staged a protest march in Sacramento against the Common Core, demanding a return to previous tests.

The phone interrupted Carl's reading.

"Hello, Carl Grinder speaking."

"Carl, Marvin. Have you read the article about Elizabeth Factor? Check the international section of the *Times*. We could all be up shit creek."

"What happened?" Carl panicked. "Also, can you send me money to pay these Booker T. Washington teachers? They're even coming to my apartment with demands."

"The Booker T. Washington schools may be broke," Marvin replied. "I'm trying to find out what happened with the teacher robot. It's possible that it went all right, and we don't have to worry about Factor's death."

"Death!" Alarmed, Carl began leafing through the paper to find the article. "Does this mean the Common Core Fund is bankrupt?"

"The article doesn't say," Marvin replied. "It only says she died on the street while running. It might not have anything to do with the robot or the fund."

Carl found the article, which simply stated that Elizabeth Factor, the head of an investment firm, collapsed while running and died, in Beijing, and that the cause of death was being investigated.

Panicked, Carl dialed the Chicago offices of the Fund and received the message, "This is the Office of the Common Core Fund. There is no one available to take your call at this time. Please leave a message, and we'll get back to you."

As Carl was phoning the Common Core Fund offices, Agent Geary was boarding a plane to go to the Philadelphia offices of Stop Testing.

He had seen the article about Factor's death and wondered about Chinese involvement, because she had been found outside the Party's compound. Limited by not having electronic communications, he wondered about the teacher robot demonstration.

The Philadelphia Stop Testing office was on a seedy section of Broad Street near the Convention Center. Walking up to the third-floor offices, Tim was greeted by a poster on the door showing a monkey, dog, goldfish, seal, penguin, and elephant lined up in front of a desk with an official-looking human. He stood pondering the poster's meaning while reading the caption: "For a fair selection, everybody has to take the same exam: Please climb that tree."

Reminding him of the morning's news article on the Common Core prison riots, another poster on the wall next to the door showed how high-stakes testing feeds the school-to-prison pipeline.

The office was one room, with a white man in his early forties dressed in a 1960's-style black cotton turtleneck and black pants sitting behind a wooden desk and two college students working at computers on a metal table near the wall. The room was covered with posters denouncing every aspect of standardized testing. One poster that caught Tim's eyes showed dollars flowing into the top of a building labeled Brightstone, with tests flowing out of schoolhouse doors. The caption at the bottom read, "Capitalist Greed Takes Over Our Schools—Stop Corporate School Terrorism."

"Interesting poster," Tim said, introducing himself to Ned Blackburn, a former high- school history teacher turned test activist. "Do you have any gripes with Brightstone?"

"They're making a fortune off schools. Public schools are struggling to financially survive, while the state and local authorities pay big bucks for these useless tests."

"I'm investigating the poisoning of US Secretary Blanchard and the Cincinnati School bombing," Tim explained.

"Are we suspects?" Blackburn suddenly looked ashen.

"We have records," Tim said, after explaining the investigations access to NSA data, "of e-mails between your members making disturbing comments about the secretary. Also, your organization poured acid on tests in Texas, hijacked an armored truck in Chicago and kidnapped the driver and guard, and threw tomatoes at the Secretary Blanchard in Atlanta, with some of your members being arrested."

"Those were local groups," Blackburn explained. "I didn't organize those events, nor did I attend them."

"But your office did approve them, and you did supply the local group with PDF files to print leaflets."

Looking down at his notes, Tim said, "Homeland Security found one of your posters linking family income to test results." Tim paused, thinking the relationship was probably true. "Meaning the head of Homeland Security thinks the poster is anticapitalist and could result in class warfare."

"Class warfare." Blackburn laughed. "You government people are so out of touch with reality. Who could imagine class warfare in this oppressed country?"

"Oppressed country? Please explain," Tim asked, secretly agreeing with Blackburn.

"The schools brainwash these kids. Before all this business about standards and testing, at least a few teachers had the opportunity to teach students the truth. Now the test dictates what they teach. Who controls the test controls the minds of American children."

"You organized students who failed the state math test into a so-called zombie march on the Minneapolis school-board building. The governor had to activate the National Guard because of potential violence. Your organization doesn't seem like a bunch of pacifists."

"Again, that was a locally organized march," Blackburn replied. "We didn't have anything to do with it. However, the idea was great, and we're asking other locals to consider it."

"Did your organizations have anything to do with California prison riots?"

"I read about that this morning. Wouldn't it be great if our organization could connect with those prison gangs? I am a little leery about working with the Aryan Brotherhood."

"So you think it's all right to work with violent criminal gangs?" Tim asked, wondering why Blackburn would say something like this to an FBI agent. But he had interrogated suspects in other terrorist cases who were so sure of the righteousness of their causes they were willing to say anything.

"We don't support violence," Blackburn quickly replied. "But many of those gang members probably failed the tests in school. Did you see our school-to-prison poster outside the door?"

"But you express a willingness to work with these prison gangs?

"Look," Blackburn stood up. "We're fighting a capitalist class determined to take over the schools to line their pocketbooks. Brightstone and Kiwi are out there harming our students with tests, made-up standards, and technology. We need all the allies we can get."

"So you would be willing to work with them?

"Not the Aryan Brotherhood; they're too racist. But the Nuestra Familia and the Black Guerrilla Family might be okay; they're trying to help minority kids. I thought that story was great about them hijacking Brightstone tests and helping kids cheat."

"So you think cheating is okay." Tim began writing down his suspicions about Blackburn being the terrorist.

"You don't want to cheat poor people or those in need," Blackburn replied, thinking the FBI agent agreed with him. "But certainly you want to try and cheat capitalist exploiters like Brightstone and its tests."

"Have you ever been to China?" Tim asked.

Blackburn looked surprised at the question. "Why do you ask? With your NSA data, you probably know that two years ago I went with a study group sponsored by the Confucius Institute. They function like our government—just a bunch of political bullshit."

"What contacts did you have while in China?"

"Contacts? They kept us isolated on the outskirts of Beijing. I never met anyone that wasn't some kind of worker for the Confucius Institutes."

"Do you know anything about teacher robots?"

"Last week, when I was visiting some teacher-union people in New York, they mentioned that Kiwi was trying to make a teacher robot to replace humans. If they do that, the capitalist bastards will really be running the schools."

"Who would be on the top of your list of suspects in the poisoning and bombing?" Tim looked closely to see Blackburn's reaction to the question.

"It would be hard for me to guess," Blackburn responded. "There is so much anger out there about what's happening."

"Do you think any member of your organization would be angry enough to do it?"

"Look," Blackburn said, sitting back down. "I know what you're trying to do. You're the FBI, and you actually represent our enemy the government. I can't speak for our members. We are loosely organized, without a central command. My office just passes on information, flyers, and possible anti-testing methods. We're sort of an anarchist group."

"If you're anarchists, why do you support public schools? Aren't they just an arm of state power?" Tim fondly remembered the great course he took on communism, anarchism, and fascism at Michigan State. Recalling a classroom debate in the course, Tim asked, "Didn't Stirner warn back in the nineteenth century that schools were the new method of political control by the nation-state?"

"How'd you know that?" Blackburn was obviously surprised by the question.

"Read him back in college," Tim replied. "We discussed Stirner's ideas on schools. I always thought he was wrong. But I gather you don't."

"You're right." Blackburn smiled. "Schools can function as instruments to control minds. The one advantage US schools had was local control and unions that protected tenure to ensure diverse ideas in schools. That's gone with the Core and state tests. Now the rich control what's going into kids' minds."

"You're willing to work with prison gangs to defeat government mind control?"

"I didn't actually mean that I would work with them." Blackburn was obviously nervous at this suggestion. "I think one reason—and again look at our poster outside—they're in prison is because the schools fail them. Without a high-school education, it's hard to get a job. Push them out or test them out, it's all the same thing—a pipeline to prison."

"And charter schools—how do you feel about them?" Tim asked.

"At first I supported them for promoting diversity in what was taught. But now they've become segregated and get around civil-rights laws."

"I'm going to wrap this up, so that I can take the next train to Washington." Tim had decided during the interview that Blackburn and Stop Testing were prime suspects, and he wanted to report the interview to Homeland Security. He also wanted to hear how the teacher robot had done in China.

Chapter 19

The receptionist told Agent Geary that Secretary Olsen wouldn't be free for an hour. So Tim wandered down to Floyd Henderson's data-mining operation. He found Floyd in a large room, sitting in front of a bank of computer monitors, while dozens of assistants worked at other computers.

"Hi," Floyd greeted Tim. "I was just thinking of you. I got information on those two Cincinnati teachers and some on Elizabeth Factor's death. Did you hear about that?"

"Read about it in the morning paper. Anything on the teacher-robot experiment?" Tim asked.

"We'd better go to the safe room to talk about this. Are you seeing Alan?"

"Later; he's busy now. I do have a prime suspect I need you to look into," Tim said, leading the way out of the office and to Homeland Security's safe room.

"One of the Booker T. Washington teachers you asked me to look at," Floyd began, after they sat down at the conference table, "has some interesting connections. There's really nothing on Blanch Cooper. She's had an ordinary life of early marriage and divorce and is active in an evangelical church. Eric Somers, on the other hand, was, as a high school-student, a member of the Skinhead Division of the Church of Jesus Christ Christian-Aryan Nations."

"He was a skinhead," Tim repeated, amazed at the information.

"He continues to have some connection with the main organization. But we've had some trouble reading his e-mails and text messages. He's using several different phones and providers, along with a variety of e-mail accounts under different names. The messages we've been able to locate are in a simple code, which was easy to break. One of them suggests he is responsible for distributing that white-power comic book."

"Do you think he should be a major suspect?" Tim asked.

"There's nothing in what we've read suggesting anything related to the bombing or poisoning. My assistants are now accessing all his accounts and phone servers to read and listen to all his conversations. I'll let you know."

"It's hard to believe that a skinhead became a teacher," Tim commented.

"Frankly," Floyd said, "all these racist organizations make me sick. It's hard for me to read their stuff."

"What about the teacher robot and Elizabeth Factor?" Tim was eager to hear what had happened in Beijing.

"We've been reading all communications within China and the United States about these two events. Let me first explain what's suspicious about Elizabeth Factor's death."

"I thought there was something funny when her body was found outside the Communist compound," Tim observed.

"We don't know exactly what happened. Witnesses say they saw her running. But she was not simply out jogging through Beijing streets. She was found wearing a business suit and loafers—hardly the outfit for jogging. The loafers were so poorly suited for jogging that the Chinese police reported her feet were actually bleeding."

"Do you think the Chinese were involved?" Tim asked.

"We can't find a connection. But one suspicious factor is that she had heart and lung problems. We read her medical history, and this was not a woman who should be jogging through the smog-filled streets of China. We're having trouble getting more information, because Chinese officials have abandoned electronic communications for calligraphy. I'll let you know if we find out more."

"What happened with the teacher robot?"

"Again, our data on official Chinese reaction is limited. We've been relying on reading e-mails from Brightstone and Kiwi officials who attended the meeting and listening to their phone conversations."

"So, what happened?"

"Apparently it was a disaster, with the robot's head spinning off and injuring students. It's hard to understand exactly what happened. All the communications have been somewhat hysterical, to say the least. The Kiwi and Brightstone executives are predicting the end of their careers and both companies."

"The head spun off." Tim laughed. "This was what the culture wars were all about. Was it a Confucius or Uncle Sam head that hit the students? I know a lot of teachers are going to like this news."

"We're applying analytic software to all the data we have for both companies and the Common Core Fund to determine the future consequences of the robot's failure. At this point, all I can say is that it looks like a house of cards collapsing."

"How are the Chinese reacting?"

"We're limited on the data. But there were two CIA agents present," Floyd explained. "A special courier will bring their written reports this afternoon. We did send our findings to the State Department and the CIA's Washington headquarters. The only thing we've heard from them is that the robot's failure is a serious blow to American interests in the culture wars."

"I need to ask you about Stop Testing," Tim said. "It is now my prime suspect, along with its Ned Blackburn. Have you found out anything new about the organization, and what about Blackburn?"

"We've been working on that since our last meeting and came up with some interesting stuff on Blackburn," Floyd answered, standing up. "Wait here for a minute, while I go get his file from my office."

As Floyd went for the folder, Alan Olsen came into the safe room.

"I guess Floyd has filled you in on the latest from China," Alan said, sitting down across from Tim. "What have you found out?"

Tim told Alan about his suspicions regarding Stop Testing and Blackburn. He also asked what Alan thought would be the consequences of the failure of the teacher robot and Factor's death.

"I just came from a CIA briefing," Alan replied. "They're waiting for the written report from their China agents, but at this time they think the Chinese were involved in killing Elizabeth Factor. They think it was murder."

"How did they reach that conclusion?" Tim asked.

"The main reason is the body being found outside the Communist compound. Also, she wasn't dressed for running and had a history of heart and lung problems. The CIA thinks the report of bleeding feet could be signs of torture. The State Department is now trying to figure out what to do if it was murder and torture."

"Here's the information on Blackburn," Floyd said, nodding his head at Alan as he reentered the room.

"Is this about Stop Testing?" Alan asked.

"I just came from Philadelphia and an interview with the group's leader. I consider him a prime suspect," Tim explained. "The head of the organization, Ned Blackburn, is an anarchist who says he would be willing to work with prison gangs to achieve his goals. As we discussed, this organization has a violent history."

"His past would support that conclusion." Floyd opened Blackburn's folder. "He was born in 1969 to parents who were self-proclaimed anarchists arrested for working with the Weathermen."

"Was that the underground anti-war group responsible for all those bombings?" Tim asked.

"When he was two, according to our data, he was admitted with severe leg burns to the emergency room of Bellevue Hospital in New York. A police report suggests the burns were from a house explosion in the West Village, where he lived with his parents. Supposedly,"

Floyd continued, "his parents were working with bomb material that caused the explosion."

"Were the parents arrested?" asked Alan.

"Blackburn's parents snuck him out of Bellevue the next day. They were later connected to the bombing of a math building at the University of Wisconsin. Canada reported they sought political asylum because of the Vietnam War."

"What happened to their kid while they were living underground?" Tim asked.

"We've mined a lot of data about the Weathermen." Floyd glanced through the folder. "Their network for hiding people was quite extensive. In fact, the New York City police department is using the Weatherman model for their witness-protection program. Ned Blackburn grew up in this underground network surrounded by violent people wanting to do harm to the United States."

"Did he go to school? When did he emerge from the underground?" Tim was becoming more convinced he was right in suspecting Stop Testing and Blackburn.

"In 1982, at the age of thirteen, his name appears on the attendance rolls of a Portland, Oregon, middle school."

"You have 1982 middle-school attendance records," Tim said in amazement.

"You would be surprised with what we have." Floyd smiled. "We have hundreds of people taking old public records and putting them into our database."

"Anyway." Floyd smiled. "There are no school records before 1982. His middle-school records note that he was enrolled without any previous school records. They ran him through a battery of tests. and his performance was way above that of the average middle-schooler. He received a good education while underground."

"What about his parents?" asked Alan.

"They emerged at the same time their kid went to the middle school. The FBI had no charges to bring against them. The Weathermen were notorious for keeping secrets. Many suspect that they participated in a string of bombings, including their building in New York. But nothing could be proved."

"Did they continue their political activities after they came into the open?" Tim asked.

"They opened a coffee shop in Portland called the Anarchist Confluence—you know, the type that serves espresso and has couches and reading materials. In other words, Blackburn spent his early years living underground surrounded by bomb-making terrorists and then aboveground with his parents running a coffee shop distributing anarchist materials."

"And later did he continue his parents' work?" asked Alan.

"At the University of Oregon, he founded an anarchist group that became active in ecoterrorism, trying to stop logging and protecting salmon streams. He was arrested and let go when he tried to blow up a dam that was blocking a salmon stream. There wasn't enough evidence against him."

"How did he end up at Stop Testing?" Tim asked.

"It's a long story, which you can read in this folder." Floyd pushed it over to him. "He became a high-school teacher in Portland and joined national radical education groups. He moved around the country and founded Anarchists for a Free Education, which tried to operate free schools like Summerhill. When the testing issue came up with the push for standards, he founded Stop Testing."

"Okay," Alan said to Tim, "go after this guy. He sounds like he could be the one."

Across town, Felicia Cochran was meeting Union President Justin Schuster and Superintendent Bill Conklin about launching a national campaign to save public schools.

"Felicia," Justin said, "I think your committee needs a little more support. I've been authorized to give you enough money to hire the best public-relations firm to sell schools to the public."

"It's got to be more than just selling schools," Bill said. "The superintendent's group thinks it should be more focused on the enemies of public schools. All the ads and media attention given to educational technology and charter schools convey a message that these will save schools. They fail to distinguish supporting public schools and corporate privatization. We should expose the attempt by these companies to line their pockets with taxpayers' money."

"I can envision," Felicia said, "TV spots showing the amount of money going from local school budgets to buy new technology and pay for services to meet Common Core Standards. Justin, do you think the union is willing to go after the sacred cow of American business?"

"We have to if we're going to survive. We may not even have a union if teacher robots take over," he answered.

"What's the word on the robot?" Bill asked. "I heard they were testing it in China."

"I don't know, but we need to hit corporations hard. Kiwi is a perfect example. They issue a stockholder report listing their earnings," Justin urged. "We should make it public and get on talk shows about it."

"It's hard to imagine much of an audience for discussing a stockholder report," Felicia observed. "We need to do something dramatic."

"What'd did you have in mind?" Bill asked. "Remember, many of the superintendents are pretty conservative."

"We can't worry about the conservatives," Justin said. "We can't please everyone, and if we don't do something, students will be attending corporate-operated schools or doing their work at home using Brightstone and Kiwi products. The corporations will take a big chunk out of public-school funds for their profits, and less money will be spent on directly on instruction."

"We should look at history and identify the best methods to change America," Felicia said with her schoolteacher tone. "Abolitionist actions sparked the Civil War and ended slavery, mass demonstrations gave women the right to vote, sit-ins and standing up to authorities ended segregation, and tearing down Pentagon fences and a little violence ended the Vietnam War."

"You think we should be like John Brown, hacking up proslavers and trying to capture federal arms at Harpers Ferry, or the Weatherman, bombing university buildings?" Bill laughed. "We could organize teachers to storm Brightstone and Kiwi."

"I'm thinking of a national teachers strike against corporatization of schools," she said. "We could get the media attention on these issues. Also, we could have teacher pickets try to shut down Brightstone and Kiwi's operations."

"I can't imagine all the teachers participating in a national strike," Bill said, "or my fellow superintendents."

"We've got to create a sense of crisis, and I think the teacher robot will work," she continued. "We must start bombarding teachers with information on the threat of the teacher robot."

"Plus," Justin said, "I think most parents will not want their children taught by a robot."

"Do we have enough money for a movie?" Felicia asked the union president.

"Movie—what did you have in mind?"

"The movie doesn't have to be subtle. It could be a spoof on the idea. Think of a movie where all the teachers are replaced by robots and one robot goes crazy in a classroom, killing all the children. We could ask Arnold Schwarzenegger to be the voice of the killer teacher robot."

"Laid-off teachers could be the heroes and subdue the killer robot. I wonder if Sylvester Stallone would be a hero teacher. It would be a big draw if those two punched it out." Bill smiled.

"I don't know if we have enough to pay big stars, but it is possible to do a low-budget film," Justin said. "I can imagine action figures with a demented-looking robot teacher and a heroic-looking teacher. We might be able to get fast-food outlets to give them away with hamburgers."

"The goal of the movie and action figures, which I think is a good idea," she said, "is to plant the idea that corporatization of schools is evil. In the movie we could show parents rallying around human teachers and joining picket lines to fight corporate evil."

"In fact," Bill said, warming up to the idea of a movie tied to a national teacher strike, "the ads for the movie could also carry our message. Think of a movie poster showing a drooling robot ripping a blouse off a female teacher with one hand while its other hand is in a cookie jar of money labeled Public Schools."

"Teachers could use the movie poster as a picket sign," Justin said. "It would be a great to billboard to put outside Kiwi. What about putting the image on buttons, along with the words, 'Save Public Schools from Corporations'?"

"The movie, national teacher strike, action figures, and this political button will certainly get us in the press and on TV," Bill observed. "Felicia, this is great. Many superintendents won't like the national strike, but they'll like the action figures for their offices and kids. Maybe we could have many action figures with different heroic teachers and representatives of the evil trying to destroy public schools."

"Felicia, one last thing before we end the meeting," Justin said. "Are you willing to move to Washington? We need you here to organize the national strike and plan the movie and action figures."

She immediately thought of Tim and answered, "I'm going to have to think about making that big of a move."

Chapter 20

The phone awakened Carl Grinder from his afternoon nap.

"Hello," Carl said sleepily.

"This is Rose Kelly; I am a nurse at the University of Cincinnati Hospital emergency room. Your wife asked me to call you.'

"Cherry!" Carl sat up, fully awake. "Has something happened?"

"She's all right—just some minor cuts and bruises. She wants you to pick her up."

"What happened? Of course, I'll be right over."

"There was an incident in front of the Freedom Center," Rose answered. "She'll explain it to you; plus, it must be all over the media, from the number of TV cameras and reporters we've had here."

Carl turned on the TV news while getting dressed and chugging down a quick cup of instant coffee.

"We're standing in front of the National Underground Railroad Freedom Center, where earlier there was a clash between the Center's director Cherry Grinder and her staff and a group calling themselves Skinheads for Racial Justice," said *Channel 12 Action News* reporter Helen Williams, shown with a Center's staff member next to her.

"According to witnesses," the reporter continued, "Around eleven o'clock this morning, the Skinheads for Racial Justice began gathering in front of the Freedom Center and marching in a circle around the entrance, waving signs and calling for racial justice for whites. The situation remained peaceful, until a busload of high-school students arrived to tour the Center."

"We have a Freedom Center staff member, Abigail Grimes, with us, who will explain what happened next." The reporter turned slightly, holding a mic in front of a tall, thin, black woman who Carl recognized from occasional Freedom Center parties Cherry held for her staff.

"So, Abigail, what happened when the bus arrived?"

"I was working the reception desk at the entrance, where I can see through the front doors. The skinheads were marching in circles, waving their awful signs. When a bus dropped off the students, the skinheads formed a line, blocking the entrance to the building shouting, and used the 'N' word."

"Did the students react?"

"Most of the students were black, and their teachers kept them near the bus. I guess the teachers were afraid of what might happen."

"What did you do?' the reporter asked.

"I phoned upstairs to my boss Cherry Grinder, describing the scene," Abigail answered.

"Then what happened?"

"Ms. Grinder came downstairs with a couple of other staff members and went out front to talk to the skinheads, and I called the police."

"Did the skinheads attack the Center's director?"

Carl gasped, hurrying to gather his car keys and wallet to get to the hospital. My God, Carl thought to himself, who could imagine that these things are still happening in the twenty-first century?

"First, Ms. Grinder tried to talk to them into letting the high-school students into the Center," Abigail explained. "Then the skinheads began to shout the 'N' word and pointed the tips of their signs at Ms. Grinder, making stabbing motions. Then they began singing some kind of song in German. I recognized it was German from college but couldn't understand the words, except for the occasional English words, 'Let's have racial justice for whites.'"

"What happened next was captured on a cell-phone video recorder," Williams said. "Abigail, as we play this video, please explain what you saw."

Channel 12 began playing a grainy cell-phone video showing a group of high-school students charging a crowd of young men with shaved heads wearing laced black boots and blue jeans held up by red suspenders. Under the suspenders were white T-shirts displaying swastikas and the words "White Power." Fists and boots could be seen flying as the demonstrators clashed.

"I guess the teachers couldn't control the students when they heard the 'N' word and read the signs. The students tried to push through the demonstrators to get to the entrance. I could hear them shout something like, 'Let us in, honkies, or you'll regret it.' That's when I saw our boss fall to the ground."

"You mean Cherry Grinder, director of the Freedom Center. You saw her fall and then what?" the reporter asked.

"It was awful. A couple of skinheads kicked her, and one shoved a sign in her face. Some staff members tried to help her up, but they were knocked over by the fighting. Then the police arrived and, I guess, called for ambulances and reinforcements."

The TV camera panned in on the reporter's face. "There are numerous high-school students and demonstrators being treated at local hospitals. The police have not made any arrests but continue to investigate the incident. Cherry Grinder, director of the Freedom Center, is being treated at the University Hospital. At this time, she is not available for comment. This is Helen Williams reporting for *Channel 12 Action News* in front of Cincinnati's Freedom Center."

"You son-of-a-bitch," Cherry said, as Carl helped her into the car. She had sustained bruises on her legs and arm and cuts on her face, and it was difficult for her to walk. "This wouldn't have happened if you hadn't gotten involved with that Common Core Fund and had money to pay your teachers."

She handed Carl a note that was shoved in her hand as she had lied on the sidewalk, wondering if she would survive.

The note said, "You better pay your teachers their next month's salary, or this is only the beginning."

"We did give Blanch and Eric a month's salary. I don't know if we'll have anything for next month. There are also the other teachers." Carl slid into the driver's seat.

"I noticed Eric Somers standing at the edge of the crowd, watching," Cherry said. "The note must be from him. I'm wondering if he has anything to do with these skinheads."

"I can't imagine Eric being friends with them," Carl replied, backing out of the parking spot. "I won't hire a racist teacher for a school like Booker T. Washington."

"Did you give him a racial litmus test? How did you know if he was racist or not?" Cherry asked.

"I guess I didn't. I just thought anyone wanting to work there would be interested in helping black kids."

"Maybe they just needed a job and money," Cherry suggested. "You should give this note to the police."

"I'll give it to that FBI agent, Geary," Carl said, pulling into the street. "I don't trust the Cincinnati police. I hear some are racists and probably support skinheads."

* * *

The day of the skinhead protest, Agent Geary took the morning train back to Philadelphia after he and Felicia had managed to spend a night together at the Willard Hotel near the White House. An arrest warrant for Ned Blackburn was issued when Henderson's crew listened to phone conversations between Blackburn and Ohio members of Stop Testing. The plan was for Tim to stop by Philadelphia's FBI office to pick up other agents, in case there were problems. Staring out the train window at the swiftly passing landscape, Tim pondered the union's request for Felicia to move to Washington.

"Did you ever threaten Secretary of Education Blanchard?" Tim asked after they had surprised Blackburn in the Stop Testing offices and brought him to the Philadelphia FBI offices for questioning.

"This is absurd. You can't stick me with the killing. I was here when it happened." Ned looked nervously at Tim. "I want a lawyer."

"If you answer a few simple questions, we'll let you go. If you want a lawyer, we'll have to hold you overnight," Tim explained, hoping to delay the appearance of a lawyer. "At any time during this questioning you can again request a lawyer, and we will get you one. Or, do you have your own lawyer?"

"I've nothing to hide. I can't afford a lawyer. Public defenders never helped my parents. I'll answer your questions so I can get out of here. But I will ask for a lawyer if I think one's needed. Go ahead; I saw my parents go through this all the time with the FBI. You guys are just full of bullshit." Ned sighed and leaned back in his chair.

"My question was, did you ever threaten Secretary Blanchard? I mean threaten him with bodily harm."

"Of course not; I'm a pacifist."

"We listened to many phone calls between you and Ohio members of Stop Test in which you said hostile things about the secretary."

"Of course; Secretary Blanchard was a major advocate of increasing testing in schools." Ned smirked. "We didn't say anything different than did the thousands of people around the country protesting against standardized testing."

"You made frequent phone calls to an A. J. Sims, a teacher in the Dayton schools."

"You actually have recordings of those old phone calls? You people are creating a totalitarian state. I guess the Common Core and tests are your methods of mind control. Welcome, 1984."

"Did you make those calls to Sims, and did you discuss Secretary Blanchard's visit to Dayton?"

"Sims has written more against testing than any person in the country. He's been on the editorial pages of all major papers. Of course we talked about Blanchard's visit. But Sims didn't think he had enough people to hold an effective protest."

"You also talked to Sims about charter schools. According to your e-mails and phone conversations, you were working on a plan to stop charter schools. Tell me about your communications regarding the Booker T. Washington Charter School Network."

"I see where you're going with this." Ned sat up. "I better have that lawyer. I'm through answering questions."

"Of course, you have a right to a lawyer. You will be processed into the federal justice system and held until a bail hearing. Our prosecutors will recommend that you be denied bail, because this is terrorist investigation. You will have a lawyer assigned to you tomorrow, or you are free to hire your own."

* * *

"What are we going to do?" Li Luan's assistant Wang Lin asked him as they walked together around the lake in the Communist Party's compound the day after Sally2's head had spun off.

"We may have some big problems. I told Mary after the meeting that I would need more money to pay the generals to keep the Jinan plant open. She said the Phillipson Foundation was probably broke with the failure of Sally2, and that Elizabeth Factor's suddenly running out of the room and dying was probably a sign her fund had collapsed."

"The Hanban office contacted me this morning," Lin said. "They're pretty upset about Sally2 and blame us, and somehow they know about the virus and Confucius chip. They want the generals to take over the Jinan plant and start producing Chinese teacher robots. Why bother, they said, trying to combine American and Chinese culture in one robot."

"The very idea of putting the two cultures together probably drove Sally2 insane." Luan laughed.

"Having the generals take over the plant might be one way out of bribing them," Lin suggested.

"I don't think the takeover of the plant will be a problem for Kiwi or the American government," Luan said thoughtfully. "If the Common Core Fund actually did collapse, then Kiwi and Brightstone are in serious financial problems. Kiwi will probably be happy to get rid of it. Of course, the generals and party officials will miss that money coming from the Phillipson Foundation."

"The Hanban had some specific ideas about the robot. They want it called Wen-Chang, after the god of learning. At first they want to send the robot to schools serving Chinese workers in Africa and South America. They're afraid these workers will lose their Chinese culture and language. Wen-Chang should be programmed to teach in Chinese and to be able to perform Chinese dances and maybe an opera."

"Do an opera!" Luan giggled. "Can you imagine a robot doing a Chinese opera? Would it be a revolutionary opera, with the robot looking like a freedom fighter, wearing a People's Liberation Army uniform?"

"Party officials like the Hanban's plan and want to get the robot working before the Japanese," Lin informed him. "We might be in a culture war with the Japanese and not the Americans."

"And after using the Wen-Chang robot with overseas Chinese, what do they expect to do with it?" Luan asked.

"Party officials want to the Wen-Chang robot to teach our minority populations. They think it might end the problems we're having with the Tibetans and Uighurs—maybe keep the Tibetans from burning themselves up."

"I guess we'll still have our jobs," Luan commented.

"If Wen-Chang proves effective in changing Tibetan and Uighur cultures and in working with Confucian Institutes, then it will be released to the world to turn everyone into Chinese."

"Next, Party officials will want to send the Wen-Chang robot up in a space capsule." Luan smiled at the idea. "Imagine the Chinese god of learning circling the earth and spreading the greatness of our culture."

Chapter 21

"What's wrong, Joyce?" asked Felicia, entering the union office after returning from Washington to find her executive secretary, Joyce Murdoch, in tears. It was the morning of the day of the skinhead demonstration at the Freedom Center.

"Bob just called and said everything is over," Joyce answered.

"You mean Bob Carlson, that guy from Kiwi you've been seeing."

"He's lost his job, and the whole plan for a robot operations degree at Horton is scrapped."

"What happened?"

"The teacher robot failed in China, and Kiwi's going broke."

"The robot failed! That's great news. But I understand you're disappointed."

"Now I'm stuck with this credential and no teaching job."

"You have this job, and there will be more teaching jobs if our plan works. But what about Bob—will you ever see him? What happened to Kiwi and the robot?" Felicia asked.

"Bob said the robot went crazy and hurt kids. Kiwi's future depended on it. Kiwi's president Phillipson was there and immediately called back to the States to shut down operations."

"They're a big company. Why did everything depend on the robot?"

"Kiwi's money was entangled with something called the Common Core Fund," Joyce answered. "Bob said the fund collapsed when the robot failed, and the fund's leader died in Beijing. Maybe killed by the Chinese."

"Will you and Bob still see each other?"

"He can't afford to fly all the time. With Kiwi laying him off, he might move to Cincinnati. But he says it would be easier to find his type of work in California. He wants me to move there."

"What do you think of living in California?" Felicia asked. "Not a bad place."

"My parents are going nuts over the idea. They're convinced all Californians are sex perverts, gay, or crazy. It all comes from our pastor, who keeps painting this Sodom and Gomorrah image."

"Did Bob say anything about Brightstone? They were with Kiwi in robot development." Felicia sat down and turned on her computer to immediately write an e-mail to Superintendent Bill Conklin and Union President Justin Schuster.

"Nothing, except that he can't get a job with Brightstone, because they're in financial ruin."

"Dear Justin and Bill," Felicia wrote in her e-mail, "I've just heard that the teacher robot failed and that the Common Core Fund, Brightstone, and Kiwi are facing financial problems. We'll need to discuss this."

* * *

In Chicago, the Common Core Fund staff stopped answering phone calls and e-mails when they heard the news. The vice president of the fund, Peter Carlisle, called their lawyer to alert him to the impending problems.

"You're telling me that Factor was running a Ponzi scheme," said Max Conrad, head of Conrad, Greene, and Swayze. "Did you know about this?"

"I'm afraid I might go to jail," Peter replied, "when our investors find out they lost everything."

"How could Elizabeth be running a Ponzi scheme with Brightstone and Kiwi involved? They are major companies."

"Elizabeth promised investors in the fund a 6 percent return," Peter explained. "She took the investor's money and loaned it to Brightstone, Kiwi, and their foundations, believing that the teacher robot would earn billions."

"Did she invest the fund's money in anything else?"

"No."

"To pay the 6 percent to investors, she had to convince others to invest. The more investors she got, the more money she loaned to Brightstone and Kiwi. So what we've got," Peter said, "is that these two companies owe the fund but can't pay. All the investor's money is lost."

"You mean," Max sounded irritated, "there is absolutely no money coming from these two companies, and all the money invested in the fund was loaned to them. I'm trying to get my head around this. I've never heard of it before. This is a Ponzi scheme with a twist. Have you contacted the presidents of Kiwi and Brightstone?"

"They're in China. Also, the fund loaned the two, John Greenwood and Jack Phillipson, large amounts of money. Loans were also made to the Kiwi and Brightstone foundations. One legal problem is that the Phillipson Foundation used the money to bribe Chinese officials."

"That's a violation of the Foreign Corrupt Practices Act. I'm not sure if the Common Core Fund will be charged under the law, but certainly the Phillipson Foundation will be. Who's in charge of the Phillipson Foundation?"

"Mary Phillipson, the wife of Kiwi's president," Peter answered.

"Both she and her husband may end up in jail. You're going to have investors suing the fund to get their money back," Max responded. "We need to meet. Can you come to our offices today at noon?"

"Sure. Do you think the Securities and Exchange Commission will get involved?"

"Of course, particularly when your investors start suing."

"Do you think I'll go to jail?" Peter sounded on the verge of crying.

"I can't answer that until we meet. There is another issue—do you have enough money left to pay our legal fees? Before our firm gets involved in defending you on fraud charges and possible foreign bribery charges, we will expect a large retainer. I'm just warning you."

Oh my God, Peter thought to himself, we don't have money to pay legal fees. I'm going to jail.

* * *

What are we going to do, Jim Fielder, Chief Financial Officer of Brightstone, wondered when he put down the phone after talking to his boss in China. They would not be able to pay the Common Core Fund loans, and they wouldn't be able to borrow any more money.

He looked out his office window at the fleet of BMWs the company had bought for its top executives, borrowing from the Common Core Fund. In addition, there were Brightstone's luxuriously outfitted corporate jets. President Greenwood insisted on buying original artwork for company walls. Plus, there were the apartments the company had bought for executives in cities scattered around the world. Jim particularly liked the ones in Singapore, New York, and Paris for their lavish furnishings and large number of bedrooms to house executive families. He frequently took his own family of four on vacation trips, flying on a company jet and staying in company-owned apartments.

Jim called Sharon Ross, vice president of the Brightstone Foundation. "Sharon, I know your boss is in China, but we need to talk immediately about the financial situation with the robot disaster. You can't spend any more money. We're in big trouble."

"Is there any money?" Sharon asked. "We're funding a junket to Sitka, Alaska, for state school officials. They really like the salmon fishing, and we hoped to convince them to buy teacher robots."

"That's off the plate," Jim responded. "No robot or money!"

"We also were paying for a public-relations firm to get Professor Riesling appointed Secretary of Education. This also involves entertaining key political officials."

"You'll have to cancel that and also stop the funding of the Brightstone Chair at Horton."

"Professor Riesling's not going to like that."

"He's a jerk anyway. Full of hot air, with all his supposed scholarship. Maybe Horton will fire him. It certainly wouldn't be a loss to anyone."

Next, Jim called Jeremy King, Brightstone's vice president of sales.

"Jeremy, I assume you've heard the news about the robot."

"How does it affect us?" asked Jeremy.

"We're worse than broke. I don't know what we'll say to our stockholders. We could be investigated by the Securities and Exchange Commission for fraud. We've borrowed heavily from the Common Core Fund. I'm calling to see about sales and any revenue you might project. I'm concerned about our cash flow."

"We've been having problems."

"That's not what I want to hear. You better cancel that family trip to Paris. We'll have to sell the apartment and planes. You'll have to pay your own way, which might be a problem if we can't pay your salary," Jim informed him.

"You're kidding! It's that bad!" Jeremy gasped.

"Yes; now tell me about sales."

"We're having problems with a number of states. Some state officials told our staff that they might not be ordering any more tests. They say Brightstone is not producing a good product, and parents are complaining about too much time spent testing."

"What kind of problems?"

"I understand that at least ten states are going to sue us for faulty tests," Jeremy answered."

"We're not selling faucets or cars," Jim said. "How can there be faulty tests?"

"That professor at Horton, Philip Riesling, is in charge of making sure the tests are okay."

"We're getting him fired or at least demoted," Jim interrupted.

"Good thing; I don't know how he ties his shoelaces in the morning," Jeremy continued. "Some test questions lack any right answers, some are incomprehensible, and many were mis-scored. The sales reps tell me that even parents may sue us for errors that kept their kids from graduating."

"Any other bad news?" Jim asked. "We'll be looking for new jobs."

"Two California prison gangs hijacked our trucks and are selling the tests to parents," Jeremy explained. "Plus, they're copying them and selling them on the black market."

"Prison gangs—how did they get involved? I can't believe there's a black market for tests."

"The prison gangs are offering cheating services and franchising them around the country."

"Cheating services," Jim repeated. "What does that mean?"

"The simplest form is just giving parents and children the right answers before the test. This is the commonest method among the gangs. They also are showing teachers how to change student answers. This has been a past practice among teachers and school administrators, but now it's turned into a major illegal business."

"What will the hijackings and cheating services mean for future sales?" questioned Jim.

"It looks like a disaster for us. We've gotten a bad name from the many cheating scandals," Jeremy explained. "There's a chorus of voices claiming our test promote unethical behavior. Now with gangs offering cheating services, our faulty and poorly constructed tests, and groups like Stop Testing, we could be out of business."

"It's hard to believe that they would stop testing." Jim sighed.

"Reps tell me these factors, plus pressure from teachers unions, may lead to states scaling back the number of required tests. We could be finished."

"Teachers unions!" Jim was startled at this news. "I thought we'd poured money into media to turn the public against teachers unions."

"They are mounting a campaign against what they call corporatization of the schools."

"What does that mean?" Jim asked.

"It means," Jeremy responded, "they want to convince the public that education money should be focused on instruction and not spent on buying our products or those of other education companies."

* * *

"That was fun at the Willard," Felicia said over dinner. "I could get used to you." They had both flown back together in the morning from Washington.

"Wish we could have many nights like that?" Tim gave her a warm smile.

"Why can't we?"

"I've been thinking about the offer for you to move to Washington," Tim replied. "I don't think you should pass up the opportunity because of us. You'd just be angry making that sacrifice. It'd ruin the whole thing."

"Given a job or you, I'd always choose you."

"That's sweet, but I know many a couple where one made a job sacrifice for another, and they came to regret it." Tim shook his head, thinking about what a great opportunity it was for Felicia.

"Let's not talk about it until we finalize what we've named the Campaign to Save Public Schools." Felicia was pragmatic and just wanted to take one step at a time.

"Have you heard anything from the union head or that superintendent?"

Felicia sat back and took a sip of her wine. "We had a long discussion today by conference call. It looks like the campaign will get started in a month, with teacher rallies in New York, Chicago, and LA focusing on the money going to education corporations instead of being used for instruction. We have all the figures."

"You think you'll get media attention?" Thinking about media, Tim wondered about the media circus that would greet him in two days when Blackburn was officially charged as a terrorist.

"I think so." Felicia smiled, thinking about finding the love of her life in the man across from her. "The union is reporting the failure of the teacher-robot experiment to the press. The main thing is that few even knew it was being developed. TV news has jumped on the story and are interviewing our people."

"I wonder how parents will react to the idea."

"Talk-show hosts think there will an uproar from parents," Felicia reported. "They've a bunch lined up to comment. The robot turned out not to be a threat but a media boon for us. It's going to give us an opportunity to get our message out."

"What about corporations? Aren't they going to fight back?"

"There are rumors that the Common Core Fund collapsed and the executives of Brightstone and Kiwi are going to be arrested on fraud charges." Felicia paused and took another bite of food.

Tim reached over and stroked her hand. "Think you can get the politicians to follow?"

"Politicians are changing their minds about testing and standards. Seemed like a nice idea when it started out. With complaints about poorly constructed tests, cheating, and now with prison-gang involvement, they're singing a different tune. Plus there are the costs. Few politicians want to tell parents there's less money to instruct their kids because it's going for tests."

"Will this be part of your campaign working with politicians?" Tim began to feel uneasy, thinking that this conversation showed how much the union needed Felicia in Washington.

"The frosting on the cake will be if the presidents of Brightstone and Kiwi get arrested. Then there's the academic scandal."

"It appears that this big testing and standards expert, Philip Riesling, out at Horton, has been lying about his research," Felicia continued. "He's actually done nothing. A whistle-blower at Horton informed the union that he suppressed research showing the Common Core Standards did not increase a person's lifetime occupational chances."

"Jesus," Tim reacted, "so much money."

"No one knows what their long-term effect on learning will be. It's all been a scam. They sat around and made these things up but never looked at the effect on students." Felicia finished her wine and motioned for a refill.

"I think we should get involved."

"You mean the two of us. I thought we were?" Felicia grabbed Tim's hand.

"No, I mean the FBI. There needs to be an investigation, since these companies are stealing government money. Maybe Homeland Security."

"Are you serious—Homeland Security?" Felicia gulped her wine.

"Tests and standards without research on the long-term consequences could be considered a threat to our nation's security. How do we know it might be a plot by Russia or the Chinese to dumb down our population? Plus, there's all the cheating and prison-gang involvement."

"You think you will follow up on this?" Felicia excitedly leaned across the table and kissed Tim, knocking her wine glass to the floor.

"I've got to get back to Philly for the grand jury hearing on our terrorist. After all that's finished, then I'll try to convince the head of Homeland Security that these tests and the Common Core should be considered terrorist acts."

Chapter 22

Agent Geary parked on Harrison Ave a half block from Eric Somers' one-story, three-bedroom Cheviot home. Once an independent town, Cheviot was home to many German-Americans, with some of the older generation having participated in organized 1930s Nazi activities. Some say this Nazi tradition was kept alive in Cincinnati by the former owner of the Cincinnati Reds baseball team, Marge Schott, who, after acquiring majority interest in the team, talked about "million-dollar niggers" and expressed her opinion that Adolf Hitler was good for Germany. She denied that the Nazi armband she kept at home represented her views.

Tim could see lights in the living room as he pushed the buzzer on Eric's front door. In the background, he could hear faint sounds of marching music. No one answered the buzzer, so Tim decided to look in back. Walking to the back, he noticed basement lights, and he could see through the basement curtains a shadowy figure moving around.

Looking through the back-door glass, Tim noticed a photo of Adolf Hitler on the kitchen wall and a banner with a thunderbolt and the words "White Power." He pounded on the door, wondering if the knocking could be heard above the increasingly loud martial music.

The marching music suddenly stopped, and Tim could make out the form of someone dressed in what looked like a uniform emerging from the basement into the kitchen, calling out, "Who's there?"

"FBI Agent Tim," Tim shouted out. "I have a few questions."

"Give me a minute to put on some clothes," Eric answered, disappearing from Tim's view.

A few minutes later, wearing a bathrobe, a smiling Eric Somers opened the back door, welcoming the FBI agent. "I'd invite you in, but things are a mess. Why don't we talk out here? Why didn't you use the front door?"

"No one answered in front," Tim responded, as Eric joined him on the small stoop outside the kitchen door.

"What'd you want?"

"The principal's wife, Cherry Grinder, received this note during a skinhead demonstration outside the Freedom Center. It says, and I quote, 'I better get my next paycheck. You don't want more of this.' She claims she saw you near the entrance. As you probably know, she was injured in the confrontation."

"Booker T. Washington owes me a salary," Eric claimed, "but they say they'll have trouble paying me. Hard to believe them, since they're rich. My wife has left me, and I may lose the house."

"Homeland Security data shows your wife and two daughters left you because of violent behavior. She filed several abuse complaints against you."

"That was all nonsense. I love my wife and kids. She's crazy and reported a dispute over controlling the TV remote. It was nothing serious."

Doubting Eric's explanation, since the complaint contained hospital reports of facial bruises and kidney damage, Tim asked, "Why were you at a demonstration by skinheads who were probably twenty years younger than you?"

"Just happened to be walking by and saw Cherry Grinder," Eric responded, "and thought it would be an opportunity to remind her of my pay. I like to walk near the riverfront. I've little to do since the school closed. I still don't know why you're here, talking about my pay."

"Carl Grinder asked me to investigate your note. I have to follow through, since it is a terrorist investigation. Could we go inside and talk? I just have a few more questions, and then I'll be gone."

"Does this have to do with the bombing?"

"We've taken a suspect into custody on terrorism charges related to the bombing. A federal prosecutor is now putting together the paperwork to bring the case before a grand jury. But your note appeared before the paperwork was officially filed, so I'm required, because of the Grinders' complaint, to ask a few questions. This may be as much of a waste of time for me as it is for you."

"You caught the bomber!" Eric exclaimed. "I bet he was Chinese. Remember we told you about that Chinese box in the storage room."

"I can't talk about the suspect. I'm sure you'll hear about him on TV after the charges are brought today. There will be a news conference after the indictment."

Breaking out in smiles and acting more affable, Eric opened the kitchen door and invited the agent inside.

"All the Nazi stuff," Eric said, pointing to the walls, "was put up by my father. He belonged to the local Silvershirts in the 1930s. Many Germans living in Cheviot remain loyal to the cause. I haven't taken down his stuff for sentimental reasons."

"So you grew up in this house?"

"I owned it free and clear after Daddy's death, but I took out a mortgage when I married. Now I may lose the house. His friends use to meet in the basement, which looks pretty much the same."

"How long did he hold meetings there?"

"Until his death in 1981. He put in a good sound system to play old World War II marching music. As a kid I could hear them singing German songs."

Sitting down at the kitchen table so he could spread out his notes, Tim commented, "It says here that in high school you were active in the Skinhead Division of the Church of Jesus Christ Christian-Aryan Nations. Also, we found that you recently distributed a comic book to Cincinnati students called *White Power Comes to Midvale*. This suggests that you might be connected to the skinhead demonstration."

"Someone has to stand up for us whites," Eric said, leaning on a counter across from Tim. "You and I have been held down by these blacks for too many years. Civil rights was just an excuse for attacking whites. Imagine building a museum for the Underground Railroad and calling it a freedom center. We know the Civil War, and emancipation kept Africans from being civilized under slavery."

Tim looked warily at Eric, wondering what was under his bathrobe, since he appeared dressed when Tim had seen him come out of the basement.

"Could I take a look at your father's basement?" Tim asked. "I've always been interested WWII memorabilia."

Eric looked apprehensive when Tim mentioned the basement. Suspicious, Tim again asked about the basement and its collection.

"It's a mess; I don't ever go down there."

Having seen him in the basement walking around, Tim persisted. "I don't care if it's messy. You should see mine. Ever since I was assigned to the Cincinnati office, I've been curious about this past history. So your father marched with the Silvershirts? That was quite a group."

Visibly nervous, Eric adjusted his robe, briefly revealing to Tim what looked like a black tie and brown shirt.

"It's time for you to leave," Eric said, gesturing toward the door. "I've a dental appointment."

Looking at Hitler's picture and the white-power banner, Tim pleaded, "Just a little glimpse, or maybe I should come back. I'd like to take some photos for my WWII collection."

"I don't think so; this is family stuff." Eric opened the back door for Tim to leave.

Tim stood and put his papers back into his file, thinking that he should look at the basement and the rest of the house before he left.

"Look," Tim said, "I'm required to look at this case from every angle. We have a suspect in custody who I'm pretty sure did the bombing and poisoning. Let me just briefly look around, and I'll be out of your hair. Otherwise, I'll have to come back with a search warrant."

"Search warrant," Eric stammered. "I thought you caught the guy."

"I know it's stupid, but the FBI will have my ass if I don't turn in a complete report about this visit. They're really picky about these things."

"Okay, just a little time; I've got to get to the dentist." Eric walked over to the basement door, revealing to Tim a pair of black boots.

Tim followed Eric down the stairs into a well-lit room covered with swastika flags, old photos of men and women dressed in Silvershirt uniforms, white-power symbols painted on exposed walls, and a large poster, dominating one wall, of a large clenched fist proclaiming "Racism Saves Lives: Revolutionary Defencism."

The basement was partitioned, with two doors leading to other rooms. One of the rooms was padlocked, and on its door was a poster of a white-hooded figure on horseback, with the words "Save Our Land—Join the Klan." The other door led to a utility room with a washer and dryer, hot-water heater, and furnace.

Glancing around the room, Tim noted two tables, one with a computer and printer and another with piles of white-power comic books. His gaze lingered on the locked door.

Eric turned on the sound system, and the basement was filled with the English lyrics to a favorite Nazi song, "German Awake," which opens:

Germany, awake from your nightmare!
Give foreign Jews no place in your Empire!
We will fight for your resurgence!
Aryan blood shall never perish!

"Your father's group met here?"

"Yes," Eric answered, walking over to the computer table and opening a drawer. "This was one of his prized possessions," Eric turned, pointing an old German Luger at Tim.

"I was taught you shouldn't point a gun at someone, even if it is unloaded."

"It is loaded. Slowly, put your gun on the table."

Tim eased his revolver out of his inside pants holster and placed it on the computer table.

"Place your hands on the wall, and spread your feet," Eric ordered.

"Eric, this isn't necessary. We have the bomber. You're just getting yourself into trouble doing this."

"You think I trust you. You're an agent of a government that is destroying our white nation." He came over, still pointing the gun at Tim. "I know the FBI is after the defenders of the Aryan race."

"Eric, why are you doing this?"

"Why are you an enemy of the white race?" Eric asked as he patted down Tim.

"You think I liked working at that nigger school for a nigger principal?" Eric ran his hand down Tim's leg, looking for another weapon. "That Secretary Blanchard was just as bad, talking equality all the time, and new standards and tests, and hoping black kids can learn as much as whites. It sickened me to have to teach at a school named Booker T. Washington. Every day I went to teach, I wanted to blow it up."

"Okay, turn around," Eric commanded, finishing the pat-down.

Eric went over and turned the volume all the way up, so that the sound of "German Awake" would drown out the pistol.

"You know they'll trace me to your house," Tim warned him.

"Not worried." Eric smiled. "I've chopped up some big-time Cincinnati civil rights people here. Killed and dragged them down to my little Nazi stronghold. I butchered them like pigs and bagged their parts. Their pieces are floating down the Ohio. They're still on the missing persons list. Remember, I have the Aryan Nation behind me."

Tim swiftly moved to disarm Eric. As he grabbed the arm holding the gun, it went off, hitting Tim in the leg. Tim forced the arm to point the Luger away from himself. He then hit Eric in the face.

The blow sent Eric sprawling onto the computer table. Tim grabbed him by his bathrobe collar, wincing at the pain from the gunshot. Eric rolled out of the bathrobe, revealing his World War II Nazi Storm Trooper uniform. Tim hit him again, causing Eric's next shot to graze his left side right below the heart.

Much larger and stronger than Eric, Tim used his football body to force Eric facedown on the floor with the gun wedged under Eric. Tim landed on Eric's back and tried to force Eric's arms back, so he could be cuffed. As they wrestled, Tim heard the gun go off and felt Eric's body suddenly go limp.

* * *

"How's my hero," Felicia said, coming into Tim's hospital room with a bouquet of roses.

"Lucky to be alive," he answered, smiling, "and lucky to have you."

"The doctors say you'll be okay. One of the bullets was close to your heart." Felicia sat in the chair next to the bed and gave Tim a big kiss on the lips.

"It was stupid of me to do that alone. But when I went to his house, I thought we had the killer already, and I never suspected him."

"The media is calling you a wounded hero for finding the terrorist. And here are some presents to prove it."

Felicia opened her handbag and brought out a plastic bag, dumping the contents of teacher-hero action figures on bed.

"Just got these," she explained. "I sent a photo of you to the place that makes them. There will be action figures with your head and face. You'll join the teacher-hero action figures we're going to give out at fast-food places."

"You're kidding. I'm not much of a hero. It was stupid to have wrestled him, but he threatened to kill me. The police told me they found evidence that he was responsible for the disappearance of a number of black civil rights workers. He chopped them up and dumped the body parts in the river."

She beamed at him and ran her hand through his hair. "You will always be my hero. How do they know he did the bombing and poisoning?"

"The locked basement room had ricin and bomb-making material. He had written notes about giving an envelope of ricin to a Dayton skinhead who dressed up in a suit and passed the envelope to one of Blanchard's aides, saying it was from the president's office. The aide never thought about it being a problem and passed it on to Blanchard."

"The bombing turned out to be a problem for him." Tim winced as he tried to move his left arm and pulled at the stitches in his side. "The locked room was filled with paranoid notes worrying that a gang called the Black Spades from the Cincinnati housing projects was out to get him. He believed the Black Spades knew he was the bomber. The guy was sick. In one note, he described taking sleeping pills, because he would lay awake at night worrying about a black home invasion. In his sick mind, he thought that by telling me the Chinese did it, I would tell others and the Black Spades, and the black community wouldn't suspect him. At least I'm alive."

"And a hero," Felicia added, giving him another kiss.

"Also, promoted." Tim laughed, looking at the teacher-hero action figures scattered on the bed. "I accuse the wrong guy and arrest him. I then happen to stumble on the real terrorist and get promoted. Life is strange."

"Promoted to what?"

"You'll love this." Tim grinned. "I've been asked to head the FBI Task Force on Terrorism. I'll be moving to Washington with you. What about us marrying?"